What Any Normal Person Would Do

Suzanne Craig-Whytock

What Any Normal Person Would Do

Copyright © 2023 by Suzanne Craig-Whytock

All rights reserved. No part of this book may be reproduced in any form or by any electronic or mechanical means including information storage and retrieval systems, without permission in writing from the author. The only exception is by a reviewer, who may quote short excerpts in a review.

Interior Photography by **DarkWinter Designs**

First Printing: July 2023

Published by **DarkWinter Press**: www.darkwinterlit.com

All rights reserved.

Library and Archives Canada Cataloguing in Publication

ISBN: 978-1-7390425-0-9

DEDICATION

This book is dedicated to all the wonderful people in my life who laugh *with* me, not *at* me. Special mention to my husband Ken and daughter Kate, without whom I wouldn't have nearly as much content.

TABLE OF CONTENTS

Foreword

Introduction

Chapter 1: Things I'm Not Good At

Chapter 2: Things I'm Good At

Chapter 3: Queen Of Worst Case Scenarios

Chapter 4: The Animal Kingdom

Chapter 5: Time's A-Ticking

Chapter 6: Bathroom Tales

Chapter 7: OCD Much?

Chapter 8: Weird Signs, Weird Sayings, And Whatnot

Chapter 9: Relationships

Chapter 10: I Like To Watch

Chapter 11: Let's Get Quizzical

FOREWORD

When people say, "Laughter is the best medicine", they're absolutely correct. I started writing humour several years ago when I was embroiled in a horrible situation where I was being harassed in the workplace. The ongoing trauma spilled over into my personal life; I couldn't eat, couldn't sleep, and I was super-depressed. Then one day, something funny happened, and I sat down and wrote about it. And the entire time I was doing that, I forgot for a few minutes about how stressful my life had become, and I felt a little better. That was in October of 2014. I already had a blogsite, and I decided to use it as a form of therapy, writing humorous anecdotes about weird things every week, and that forced me to start looking at the world through a more positive lens. Eventually, I changed jobs, started working in Toronto and, aside from the commute, life became much better, but I kept writing the blog, now known as **Mydangblog**. Now, 8 years later, I'm happily retired, have several books published by two different publishers, and have launched my own literary magazine, with plans to expand into an independent publishing house where I can publish other writers and keep spreading the love. This is the first step—figuring out how to do it. So I hope that a) it all works out and I can produce this collection of satirical essays as an e-book and a paperback in order to follow the same process for other people and b) that you enjoy this experiment. Also, for the purpose of this volume, you should probably know the cast of main characters:

Husband: Ken

Daughter: Kate

The Dog: I've had several over the years; for simplicity's sake, they are all The Dog.

INTRODUCTION: WHERE IT ALL BEGAN—MY FIRST BLOG POST

Almost ten years ago, I started a blog called Educational Mentorship as a way to interact with a younger professional that I was tasked with mentoring. Once the mentorship ended, I was left with a) a bad taste in my mouth and b) a really cool, ready-to-go blog site. So I decided to change things up a little bit and turned the blog into a reflection up* the things that happened to me either in real-life or sometimes in my head, which were often even weirder, and I started referring to it as Mydangblog. I couldn't officially rename the blogsite because a) I am not that technologically proficient and I spent 15 minutes trying to reset my email for the stupid site and I still don't think it worked and b) Educational Mentorship is kind of an ironic title in a lot of ways. Despite that, I'm known around the interweb as Mydangblog or sometimes Player One (well, I wish I was known as Player One—I've been trying for years to make that nickname happen, so maybe this will be the time).

Here's where it all began...

I was in the bathroom at work drying my hands with the hand dryer (because a) I had just washed them and b) I was freezing and the heat was awesome) when I noticed a can of Febreze air freshener on top of the paper towel dispenser labelled "Alaskan Spring". So I sprayed it because I've always wondered what spring in Alaska smelled like (does it really smell kind of like stale Old Spice cologne? Has anyone been to Alaska in the spring? If so, can you clarify this?) when it occurred to me that maybe other people had used it BEFORE they washed THEIR hands, and then I got all germaphobic-y and had to rewash my hands all over again. Yep. The thesis of this story is that you should always spray room freshener in a public bathroom BEFORE you've washed your hands, then you're good to go. Or that Alaska smells like someone's grandfather.

(*Yes, I know that there's a typo in the introduction. It's there for a reason. Or maybe two reasons that are inextricably linked. While I was typing, Ken (my husband) came in and wanted to talk to me about something, I don't know what (because I was typing, you see?) Ken is always going on about how people can't really multi-task and then he was like, "Can't you listen to me and type at the same time?" And then I made the typo, which just proves that a) no, I can't multi-task and b) it's ironic that he's always telling me that I can't multi-task, then he insists that I do it.)

And that's where it all began. And now it's time to find out all about me. Are you ready?

WHAT ANY NORMAL PERSON WOULD DO

CHAPTER 1: THINGS I'M NOT GOOD AT

I Am Very Bad At Math

Of all the things I'm not good at, the number one thing would be math. Before I was born, my mother worked at a bank. My father began his career as a toolmaker and machinist. They are both good at math. My brother has a Ph.D. and is good at math along with a lot of other things. Ken is good at math. Kate is exceptional at math, having taken advanced calculus, and is able to do computer coding. Me? I am sh*tty at math. I'm like the middle of a very mathematical Venn Diagram where the middle is someone with no ability to work with numbers AT ALL, and that person is playing with a puppy and laughing at memes about cats, and if you're saying to yourself right now, "That's not how Venn diagrams work!", let me once again remind you that I AM NO GOOD AT MATH.

Once I was on the commuter train, sitting with my friend Mark, and he was mad because all the stores were now decorated for Christmas, and according to him, holidays were just an excuse to sell stuff.

"Did you know," he said, "that yesterday was National Sandwich Day?!"

Me: Did you have a sandwich in honour of this special day?

Mark: No, I did not.

Me: Personally, I prefer Pi Day.

Mark: What kind of pie?

Me: No, like 22 divided by seven. I think that's on July 22nd.

Mark: (*looks it up*) It says here it's on March 14. That's a Saturday.

Me: Ooh, then it could be a whole Pi weekend, because Pi is 3.1415. What's Pi for anyway?

Mark: I think it's to calculate the area of a circle.

Me: Why would you ever need to do THAT? Just buy enough floor tile to make a square and trim stuff away. Is it some theoretical bullsh*t thing, like Schrödinger's Cat?*

Mark: No. It's probably for things in nature, like calculating area in the ocean.

Me: Like what, how big is the Bermuda Triangle? Oh wait, that's a triangle. I think you use a different formula for that. It's the Pythagorean theorem.

Mark: Are you sure?

Me: Andre! Andre! How do you calculate the area of a triangle?

Andre, The New Train Car Attendant: You use the Pythagorean theorem.

Me: See? I told you I was good at math.

WHAT ANY NORMAL PERSON WOULD DO

Mark: Happy National Vinegar Day, by the way.

Then Ken read the above. His brow furrowed and he asked, "What are you talking about?

Me: It's the day that people celebrate vinegar, I guess.
Ken: Not that part!
Me: Oh you mean, the Pythagorean theorem. A squared times B cubed or whatnot, and some other stuff gives you the area of a triangle.
Ken: No, it doesn't! That's what you use if you don't know the length of the hypotenuse of a right-angled triangle. And it's A squared plus B squared equals C squared. Your whole train car sucks at math.
Me: Then how do you calculate the area of a triangle, if you're so smart?!
Ken: Height times base divided by two.
Me: Okay, nerd.

(*Also, Schrodinger's Cat IS bullsh*t. Once, I was watching Jeopardy, and Alex Trebek asked this one woman, "I understand you're a physicist. Why do you like physics so much?" and she said, "Because physics is always right." And I was like, "That's BULLSH*T, BRENDA. Schrodinger's Cat is not BOTH alive and dead. A cat is EITHER alive or dead, whether you can see it or not!" See, this is my issue with physics. You can't claim that just because you put something in a box, that it exists in two simultaneous states. I mean, you can CLAIM it, but just because you say something doesn't make it true. You can SPECULATE on the state of the cat, but that doesn't change the fact that a cat isn't f*cking magic. As you can see, I would have made an awesome physicist even though I'm terrible at math. And I would NEVER put a cat in a box, although if you've ever owned a cat, you know that they do love being in boxes).

And then I thought I was getting better at math, but I wasn't. We got one of those weird *Bits and Pieces* catalogues right before Christmas, you know the one where you can buy jigsaw puzzles, novelty socks, plastic garden gnomes and so on. There was this clock you could get that was advertised as a "fun" math clock, and that should have been a red flag right there. Instead of numbers to tell the time, there was just a series of mathematical equations around the dial.

Me: Hey Ken, check it out! This equation is a square root question—the answer is 2!

Ken: Obviously.

Me: What do you mean, 'obviously'? I think it's pretty good that I got the answer considering I haven't taken math since grade 11. This question here is using long division. The answer is—

Ken: Four. It's 4 because that's the number on the clock. All the answers are the numbers on the clock. See, this question is using pi…

Me: And the answer is 9. I don't even know how to do that kind of math but now I know the answer anyway. Stupid clock.

WHAT ANY NORMAL PERSON WOULD DO

Ken: So you don't want it for Christmas?
Me: How many fingers am I holding up?
Ken: The answer is 1.

But then I felt better and remembered that I used to help Kate with her math homework and that always went well:

Kate: Math, math, blah, blah, dividing by zero.
Me: Oh, that's easy. Whenever you divide by zero, you end up with the same number you started with. Like 15 divided by zero is 15.
Kate: No, it's not! You can't divide by zero.
Me: Sure you can. I have 15 things. There's zero things that go into it, so I still have 15 things.
Kate: That's NOT how it works. It's impossible. See, if I put 15 divided by zero into my calculator, it says "Error".
Me: I paid good money for that calculator—what's wrong with it?
Kate: Nothing! You just can't divide by zero.
Me: But I just did.
Kate: But you're wrong. Zero would go into 15 an infinite number of times, so it can't be calculated.
Me: But I just calculated it.
Kate: NO, YOU DIDN'T.
Me: Look. If you have 15 slices of bacon, and you try to divide them by zero, how many slices of bacon do you have left? 15! Because you have eaten zero of them!
Kate: 15 is the REMAINDER!...wait, is there bacon?

Me: Sure. Do you want 15 slices or zero?

But even though I struggle with math, I really like numbers, especially the ones in my car. In 2015, I bought a cute little car. It was a 2013 model but it had only been used for car shows and demos, so it had very low mileage; in fact, when I got it, the odometer (I just googled "thing on car that tells you mileage" in case you were thinking I was super-knowledgeable about cars) was below 2 000 kilometres, which is like 10 000 US miles or something, and I thought that was really cool. As I was driving it places, I would look at the 'odometer' every once in a while to see if I'd hit a mileage milestone and if I did, I would pull over and take a picture. I did this at 11 111, 12 345, 44 444 (All those 4s look really cool, I think. Although the number 4 is apparently unlucky to some cultures, it isn't to mine—I'm half English and half Scottish, so 4 is simply the time we have tea and haggis.)

Then I reached a scarier number, 66 661—but I didn't drive the extra 5 kilometres to take a photo, on the off-chance that it might stir up some kind of negative universal energy (as an aside, I participate in a Chinese creative writing Zoom group occasionally and the password for the room is 666, and whenever I see that number, my first instinct is to yell, "Ah! The number of the beast!" But I don't do it out loud, just in my head and usually to an Iron Maiden song. The first time I entered the password, I was worried that I would be transported into one of the 9 circles of hell, but no, it was just a group of friendly Asian people, so Dante was way off there).

Anyway, a while back, I was driving and I realized that my

odometer read 79, 972. "That's so close to 80,000," I said to myself in my head. "Only a little more than a thousand kilometres to go and I can get another cool picture." And if right now, you're saying to yourself, "I think the math is really, really wrong here," you would be absolutely correct. So I got to my destination, glanced at the odometer and gasped in dismay to see that it read 80, 007 and my first instinct was to yell "What the f*ck!" And I did that out loud, not in my head. I was well and truly furious with myself for once again being completely stymied by mathematical calculations, and I drove home in a snit. At least for the first 5 minutes, because my odometer is digital. The 8 looks like a capital B, and the zeros look like capital Os, and the 5 looks like a big-ass S and I realized, with a sudden thrill, that if I waited another seventy-some-odd kilometres, I could spell out the word BOOBS and that made me smile all the way home.

And then a few days later, I was driving to physiotherapy and noticed that my odometer read 80 041. I did some quick mental calculations and figured that I had 44 kilometres to go before I would reach the nirvana of mileage, the incredible 80085. 'There's no possible way it will take more than 44 kilometres to get to the clinic,' I thought to myself naively. And so I proceeded to drive across country, trying to reach my objective before I got to the highway where I wouldn't be able to pull over and take a picture. Unfortunately, I'm as bad at distances as I am at math, and I pulled onto the highway at 80066.

'That's okay,' I comforted myself—'there's no possible way that it will take 19 kilometres to get to my exit.' Then, after a few minutes, the odometer hit 80083. I was still two exits away from my destination, so I did what any normal person would do—I got off the highway immediately. I drove down the off-ramp, heart beating in my chest (because where the hell else would it be beating? But I do love a good cliché) as the odometer clicked to 80084. Then, like a beacon in the night, I saw a small laneway leading into a townhouse complex. I turned the corner, literally and figuratively, just as the odometer hit 80085, and slammed on the brakes. I snapped a quick picture and sent it to Ken with the caption, 'HAHA it says BOOBS!' Because I'm a grown-ass woman with a juvenile sense of humour and an indomitable will.

For most of my career, my job never involved math, which was lucky for everyone involved, but once, during the time I was working in Toronto, I applied for a job closer to home. I loved the job I already had, but it was a long commute. The new job was kind of the same as what I was doing, I thought, and to be honest, I didn't really want to change jobs immediately, but at the bottom of the job posting it said that eligible candidates would be put in a pool for future positions, and that seemed like a great opportunity. So I applied, and lo and behold, I got an email about an interview. And at the bottom of the email was a description of the interview telling me that I would have to prepare a presentation for the interview panel. On MATH. My first reaction was, "Did they even LOOK at my resume?"

Because I have a lot of qualifications and experience, none of which have anything at ALL to do with the numbers or the adding or dividing or whatnot, and the fact is, doing math can often be embarrassing for me. For example, there was the time I threw a party

WHAT ANY NORMAL PERSON WOULD DO

for Kate's 18th birthday and Ken's 50th birthday, and I decided to make a special toast:

Me: This has been a year of milestones for our family. I mean, like, since last July, not since January. A calendar year, let's say. Anyway, last year, Ken and I celebrated our 50th anniversary—

Everyone: 25th!!

Me: What? Oh right, of course. Ken's 50. We've been MARRIED for 25 years. Anyway, then I turned 50, and now Ken's turned 50 and that's really special because 25 and 25 is 50…

Everyone: ??

Me: And of course, Kate is 18 and an official adult, which is also really special, and now she's going to university. So.

Ken: Yes. It occurred to me the other day how important these connections are to us all. I look around and see these people who are so significant to our lives, coming together in kinship and love, and it's a very special thing. Thank you all for coming.

Me: Wait! I'm not done yet! Uh, Ken and I now have been together more than half of our lives, since we're both 50 and well, half of 50 is 25—wait, is that MORE than half? Regardless, it's been a wonderful first half—

Ken's Mom (dark, ominous laughter): The next half might not be as good though.

Me: Anyhow, I'm drunk.

I wasn't actually drunk, but being intoxicated was a better

excuse than being sh*tty with numbers. I learned two things that day. First, instead of winging it, you should always plan your toast carefully and ensure there is no MATH in it. Second, Ken's mom is a lovely woman but she DOES have a certain "the apocalypse is coming" vibe about her.

    Anyway, back to the job I'd applied for. For obvious reasons, I'd avoided doing math for the most part in my private life and up until a certain point, the closest I've ever come to doing math professionally was teaching Life of Pi, so when it said at the bottom of the interview description that there would be a TEST at the end of the interview, I was like, "What? A MATH TEST?!" because nowhere in the job description had it even mentioned math at all, and it seemed pretty obvious by then that they probably already had someone for the job, someone who was, perhaps, good at math. So when the place called me to confirm that I got the invite, I actually had to ask the woman, "So is the test at the end a math test?" because if it was, there was no point in going, but she said she didn't think so, that it was probably a "scenario". Which it was. And ironically, I totally ROCKED the math presentation, but I blew the "scenario" which was writing a letter in response to someone who was very angry. I responded the way I normally would—no, not by saying "Take a f*cking step back"—but in a professional way which was "Please provide more information to help me understand your anger." It turns out though, that apparently I was supposed to direct them to a variety of different websites where they could explore their feelings themselves.

    But I guess I was either traumatized or inspired because that night I had the most bizarre dream where I was teaching math to a group of kids:

Me: And that's how you figure out "less than" versus "greater than".
Student: Why is that important?
Me: Because it's the foundation for all other mathematics. Like algebra.
Student: What's algebra?
Me: Algebra is when you have to find a solution to an equation that has a missing variable.
Student: What does THAT mean?
Me: Algebra is like being a detective, but instead of solving mysteries, you're solving for "x".

Then I woke up in a cold sweat and yelled, "Is that right? How the F*CK do I even know that? What the hell is a missing variable?!"

Ultimately, as a result of the interview, I DID get put into the pool for future positions, mostly on the merit of my math presentation, which is another one of life's great mysteries.

Other Things I'm Bad At

I'm even worse at small talk than I am at math. I know I've already demonstrated my shortcomings when it comes to the numbers and whatnot, but that pales in comparison to my struggles with small talk. Here's an example. I had to get my car's thermostat replaced, so I took it to the car dealership, and they gave me a rental car, since I'm now a "VIP" by way of the fact that I've bought 3 cars from the same car guy (mostly because now I know him and we NEVER HAVE TO MAKE SMALL TALK). He's great, and he doesn't mind if I text him at dinner to see if I can test drive stuff (As a side note, I thought he was still at work, and when I realized that he was at home, I was horrified because I absolutely avoid imposing myself on anyone except my family, but he was really nice about it, and set up the test drive anyway).

Anyway, they called for a shuttle driver, who wanted to talk about the weather, and traffic, and that was okay because all I had to do was say, Mm hmm, and Right, and Really? and things like that. But then I got to the car rental place, and the rental guy was one of those SUPER-FRIENDLY people who wants to chat, and that's when things got uncomfortable. I'm kind of an introvert, and I was tired, and it was the end of a long day, so I can't really be held responsible for the verbal fiasco to come. He proudly announced that he was going to give me the "brother" to my car, so I was kind of hyped up, thinking I was getting an awesome ride because MY car is a black Chevy Sonic Turbo with a red trim kit. Then he took me outside and presented me with a Chevy Cruze. It was navy blue, and kind of scruffy. He looked at me expectantly, and I didn't know what to say, so I said, "A Cruze. My dad says it has a good engine." Then the conversation took a bizarre turn. The rental guy looked at me and asked, "Oh, does your Dad work for General Motors?" and then I became confused, (because how is that in any sense of the word, a LOGICAL connection?) and I said, without thinking, "Nuh, he's just some old guy."

I knew as soon as I said it that it wasn't even close to being an appropriate response, and to make things worse, the rental guy gave me a funny look, and said, "Okay then," in that kind of dismissive way people have, and I tried to make things better by explaining that my father was a retired teacher, etc. and not even that old, but VERY SMART when it came to cars. This, unfortunately encouraged him, and he started talking about his wife, also a teacher, and how she had to teach some students whose family got blown up on a boat (?) but I wasn't really listening and just fell back on Mm hmm, and Right, and Really? which seems in retrospect to always be the safe, non-offensive choice for someone who isn't good at small talk.

I Am Terrible At Being A Rebel

"Remember when the police called our house and said they had you in custody?" my mom asked the other day.

"Oh yeah," I said. "Not one of my finer moments."

"But you were just trying to do something nice," she consoled me.

And for the record, I wasn't ACTUALLY in police custody. In fact, I was sitting at the dinner table, completely oblivious, as my mother said, "What?!" into the phone and then gave me an ominous look. Here's the whole story:

I was fourteen and I'd just started grade 9. I was in the bathroom at school when two girls came in. I knew one of them—"Mary Jane" had been a neighbour a long time ago, and the last I'd heard, she'd gotten into some kind of mysterious "trouble" and had been sent to juvenile detention. She was tough-looking, and so was the girl she was with. But Mary Jane recognized me:

Mary Jane: Hey. How have you been?
Me: Good. How about you?
Mary Jane: Not bad. So my friend and I have a problem. We really need to get jobs and make some money because we're homeless. But we don't have any ID. If you loan us yours, we can get jobs at the Fall Fair and be able to afford a place to live.
Me: Okay. Here you go.

Yep, I handed over my Social Insurance Card, my birth certificate, AND my library card to these two girls without a second thought. Unfortunately, as it turned out, they had both just escaped from the juvenile detention centre where they had been sentenced to reside for various crimes. So they WERE technically homeless…At any rate, they used my ID to try and get jobs at the Fair, someone recognized them, and they were re-arrested. But the police were confused at first about the identity of the girl Mary Jane was with, hence the phone call to my house. And then I had to go down to the station to pick up my ID. Instead of a tongue-lashing by the cops though, I got this:

Police Officer: Are you all right? The girls said they really threatened you and made you give them your ID.

Me: What? No, they didn't. I felt sorry for them, so I just gave it to them.

Police Officer: Seriously? Because they were looking at additional charges for threatening you.

Me: Nope.

Police Officer: Then we need to have a serious discussion about what you did.

Apparently, you shouldn't give anyone, let alone fugitives from the law, your identification. Something about "aiding and abetting" was mentioned, but I don't remember much else since I was crying at that point. Part of it was because I was scared sh*tless but it was mostly because I realized in that moment that I would NEVER be a badass. And it's remained true for the rest of my life that, whenever I did something reckless, I was either too worried to enjoy it, or I got caught, which always takes the fun out of being "devil may care". Essentially, I am a goodass. Here are some examples:

1) The only time I skipped class in high school happened to be on the day of Parents' Night. I'd completely forgotten about that fact, and had spent a glorious hour in the girls' bathroom with a couple of friends, gossiping and smoking (yes, I smoked as a teenager, but in true goodass fashion, I developed asthma, so no glamourous smoking rebel life for me—just a wheezy one). Anyway, my parents came home from

Parents' Night really angry:

Mom: Where were you today during Social Studies?
Me: In class, of course, why?
Dad: Mr. McMullen wondered how you were feeling, since you were ABSENT.
Me: What? Me? No, I sit at the back—he must not have seen me…
Mom: Nice try. You're grounded.

2) When I was teaching high school, I decided one day that I was going to bring a comfy chair into my classroom. I put it on a dolly and was just wheeling it into the building when the head custodian saw me.

Custodian: No upholstered furniture allowed! They cause lice!
Me: What?
Custodian: Take it away!

Well, I was pretty steamed, and baffled by her logic regarding the lice, so I waited until the next day, and when the coast seemed clear, I enlisted another younger staff member to help me get it on the elevator to take up to my room. We loaded it, all nervous and watchful, but there was no one around. We rode up to the fourth floor. Then the elevator doors opened, and there she was, like some kind of giant wizard, waving her arms around:

Custodian: I am a servant of the Secret Fire, wielder of the flame of Anor! You shall not pass!! Take that chair to Mordor, and don't try to sneak it in again!!

Us: Yes, High School Gandalf.

Custodian: Fly, you fools.

3) A few years ago now, all the stores instituted a policy where you had to pay for grocery bags. But at the Zehrs self-checkout, the machine asked you to indicate "how many bags you wish to purchase". And so for years, I thought I was being a tiny bit of a badass by always indicating "0", because frankly, I didn't WISH to purchase ANY damn bags. I justified it by blaming Zehrs for being semantically challenged. Then, a friend pointed out that Zehrs donated the money from the bags to charity, so instead of feeling like a rebel, I just feel guilty for depriving the children, and if they didn't get toys for Christmas, it would be all my fault. So now, I always pay for one more bag than I'm actually using to make up for it.

4) When I was taking the train home from Toronto on Friday afternoons, I always had a glass of wine from the bar cart. It wasn't particularly good wine, and it cost $7 for a very small glass, but still, it was nice at the end of a long week to start early. One day, a friend at work gave everyone this new wine that came in cans. I tried it (at home, not at work) and it was actually pretty good, and not very expensive. "And the best part," said my friend, "is that it looks just like a soda can so you could drink it on the train and no one would ever know!" So that Friday, I got on the train with my secret can of wine. Then the bar cart came:

Janet: The usual?

Me: No, I'm fine thanks.

Janet (confused): Are you sure you don't want anything?

Me: Oh no, I'm good.

Janet: Hmmm. So you're not feeling well. Let me know if there's anything I can do.

I called the conductor Janet because she looked and acted just like the character Janet in that TV show "The Good Place", which is one of my favourite comedies, and our conversations usually went like this:

Me: Janet?

Janet: Hello!

Me: Can I get some wine?

Janet: Okay! Here.

Anyway, after she continued down the aisle, I surreptitiously opened my can of wine. But I couldn't enjoy it for two reasons: Janet kept coming by to check on me because apparently she thought I must be sick, so I had to keep hiding it, and second, they made the usual announcement about not having personal alcoholic beverages on the train, and I started obsessing that another passenger would see that the label on the can said 'Sauvignon Blanc' and not 'Sprite', turn me in, and I would be forced off the train in the middle of nowhere after having my sad wine can confiscated.

I suppose in the long run, being a goodass is better for me, because anytime I do something even mildly rebellious, I just worry, and it takes the fun out of it. Like whenever I'm at Starbucks and they insist on writing my name on the cup, I tell them it's 'Bob'. But the barista always gives me a dirty look, and then I feel bad, like I need to explain that I'm not mocking HIM, just his stupid store policy. The only time I truly embrace my badass side is when it comes to protecting the people I love. Once Kate's Grade 1 teacher was mean to her and made her cry, so I confronted the jerk on the playground and tore him a new one. Then I sat in a comfy chair, smoked a cigarette, and drank canned wine that I had triple-bagged. Like a boss.

The only other time I'm ever really a badass is when I'm travelling. I am a total f*cking badass when I'm travelling and here's why:

1) Despite the fact that I'm severely allergic to shellfish, I've wandered numerous ocean beaches and collected seashells. This doesn't sound dangerous, but the last time I did that in British Columbia, I picked up some shells then accidentally chewed on my cuticle (not so much an accident as part of an OCD thing), and then my lips swelled up. So now, if I want to collect seashells, I'm literally TAKING MY LIFE IN MY OWN HANDS, and have to consciously avoid putting my fingers in my mouth until I can wash with soap and water, or else risk having to use my EpiPen. I live my life on the edge, folks.

2) I am deathly afraid of heights, but I have still climbed up ruined

castle towers and stood on ramparts that were 100 feet in the air. Did I have a full-blown panic attack at Harlech Castle when I realized that I was on the top of a stone wall with no guardrails and at any moment some unruly British child could run past me, causing me to lose my balance and fall to my death? I may or may not have. (Narrator's Voice: She did). But I still crawled back to the stairs like the daredevil I am instead of crying like a big baby.

3) I defied the tide and clambered over jagged rocks to make my way to a private little alcove half a kilometre from the main beach at our bed and breakfast when we were in Wales. I had no choice really—Kate and Ken announced they were doing it, and I had to go along or be left behind to worry about them dying. I figured if I was with them, I could scout out the worst-case scenarios before one of them fell off a tippy rock or poked a jellyfish with their fingers. I spent the whole time with one eye on the ocean and one eye on the rocks that threatened to break my ankles. But we made it there, and I was glad I went with them, because who else besides me was going to shout, "I forbid you to climb that cliff!" or "That crab might not be dead so don't pick it up!"

4) On a cruise ship once, I made an old man give me a chair, all by my badass self. In fairness, I HAD the chair, and he tried to take it away, but I was like "Out of my cold, dead hands, elderly English dude!" I should probably provide a little context—on the "ship", they had trivia competitions 4 times a day, and because it was one of the few activities onboard that was actually free, EVERYBODY went. Except it was held in a small pub with limited seating, so people got

pretty testy about the chairs, especially since you could play in teams of 6 and the tables and chairs were arranged in groupings of 4. So this particular time, I asked a guy if he was using one of his chairs, and he said no. I was in the process of moving it when this big old man came over and pulled it out of my hands. Seriously. He was like, "Oh, I have this chair," and I was like, "Um, I asked for it first, but whatever," and I let go. Because I'm Canadian, and a chair isn't worth being a dick over. But my sacrificial, and slightly sarcastic attitude made him feel bad, so he gave it back to me. Score one for the good guys.

5) Driving in the UK is enough to earn anyone the moniker of 'madcap heroine'. Of course, I wasn't actually driving—I was the navigator, having never learned to drive a stick shift. I mean, why have a dog and bark, am I right? But the Brits drive on the wrong side of the road (yes it is, don't argue), and the bulk of my job was yelling at Ken "Stay to the left!" Also, the "roads" in the UK, especially in Wales aren't really roads at all, at least not by Canadian standards. What they call a major roadway in Wales is what we call a "tractor path" here. For example, the so-called road to our first bed and breakfast went through a gravel parking lot and out the other side, then became a one-lane walking path with little spots to pull over in case someone was coming in the other direction. The directions we were given said, "Go past Hunter's Fleece Cottage, then follow the track downhill for 100 yards" where there was an almost sheer vertical drop. Getting back up was a treat, with Ken gunning it in third gear and hoping to hell that no one was coming the other way. The best part was when the GPS would announce, "Take the next left onto A725" and it would SOUND like

a real road, but it would be one lane, pinned in on both sides by rock walls, and suddenly there would be sheep.

I was a kick-ass navigator until the day that Ken decided to defy the GPS and plot his own route:

Ken: I took a screenshot of the way I want to go. Where do I turn next?

Me: How do I turn the iPad on?

Ken: Push that button. Where do I turn?! I need to know now!

Me: Where's the 'You are here' arrow? How do I know where to turn if I don't know where I am?

Ken: We started from New Steddon Road. Where do I go next?

Me: The map goes sideways if I try to figure out which way is North.

Ken: I don't need North! I just need to know where to turn! God, I forgot how bad you are with maps!

Me: I'm not bad with maps! You can't just give someone a screenshot of some streets, not tell them where they're starting from, and expect them to calculate your route! I'm not a GPS, you know.

Ken: Fine, just program the GPS then.

Me: Okay. Where are we going again?

Ken: Sigh.

Kate: What's going on?

Me: Just go back to sleep. I've got this covered.

WHAT ANY NORMAL PERSON WOULD DO

Two other minor proofs of my badassedness: First, I walked through the haunted corridor of a castle. It wasn't haunted—I have plenty of experiences with ghosts, which you'll read about later, and there wasn't one there, despite the place being featured on some reality show where a woman swore there was electromagnetic energy and an angry ghost who wanted to strangle people. Second, I ate haggis. If you're Scottish, you have to. I just love being descended from a culture whose national dish is so disgusting that you have to force yourself to eat it, but you're so stoic that you do it anyway. My Scottish cousin Lynn put it this way: "I keep trying it because I want to like it, but it's so gross." So there you go. I'm a devil-may-care, throw caution to the winds kind of gal who's afraid to drink canned wine on trains.

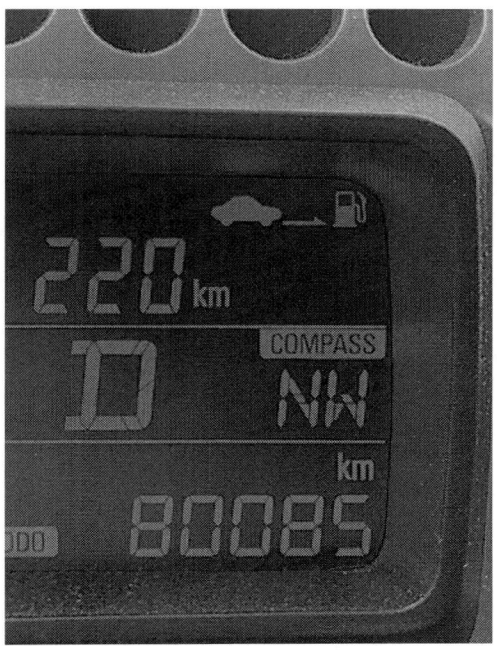

CHAPTER 2: THINGS I AM GOOD AT

Now that you've read about all the things I'm NOT good at, I'm sure you're wondering exactly what I AM good at, like what are my particular skill sets...

Organizing Heists

One Friday, I was sitting at my desk at my new job in Toronto when my phone screen suddenly lit up. I looked over, and there was a text message. I immediately stopped what I was doing to investigate, because no one ever texted me except the people I work with, and I was AT work. And I don't mean to imply that I'm unpopular or live a very lonely existence—it's just that Ken was still insisting on using Blackberry Messenger like a 90-year-old man (he's since upgraded to an iPhone that he inherited from Kate) and Kate only used Facebook Messenger, because god forbid a daughter should actually ever call her mother. As for the rest of my family, they DID call me, usually during meetings and whatnot, causing me to rush out in terror, worried that the worst has happened, only to be asked to come to dinner on the weekend.

So I sat there for a moment, pondering the possibilities, and then opened up the message. It said, "Just checking if you're available for a job." I was immediately intrigued. Of course, I already had a very good job, but I was only an "Acting" Manager, and there was always the risk that one day, I'd have to stop acting like one, and actually BECOME one. So I thought for a moment, and then wrote back, "Ooh, what kind of job?!" I'll admit that I may have sounded a little over-excited, but tone is hard over text, and I wanted to convey a sense of child-like wonder as well as tremendous enthusiasm. I waited breathlessly for a reply. Nothing. Had I overplayed my hand? Still nothing. To pass the time, I went to the website of the company that the text had come from. There were some very interesting jobs available there: Medical Sales Representative, Relationship Banker, Records Management Specialist, Unloader…I didn't know what some of these were, but they all sounded very life-fulfilling.

It was almost lunchtime, so I went to heat up my leftovers. When I came back, there was an ominous reply. "It's a warehouse job."

Suddenly, it occurred to me that perhaps this wasn't a job, but was, in fact, a "job". Was I being offered the opportunity to commit some kind of crime? And then it all made sense: Medical Sales Representative must be code for Drug Dealer. Relationship Banker? That was obviously running an Escort Agency. Records Management Specialist, I guessed, would be something akin to a Mob Accountant. Unloaders…unloaded stolen goods. What had I gotten myself into?

But then, I had a thought. I was always trying to challenge myself to try new things, things that I would never normally do. And a "warehouse job" was certainly something I'd never entertained before, but why not? I mean, I didn't know much about heists, but there were a LOT of movies out there about them, and if Sandra Bullock could do it, why couldn't I? I regularly organized and oversaw events involving more than 1500 people at a large convention centre—how hard could it be to rob ONE warehouse? And the best part was that the place I now worked had its OWN warehouse that I could practice on! But wait. The one thing I knew from watching all those heist movies was that a good warehouse job always involved a team. Luckily, I had a team, and a very efficient and intelligent team at that. And the best part was that we wouldn't need any type of weapon because they were all very fit, kind of like ninjas, if the way they snuck up on me in my office was any indication. I was getting an Oceans 8 vibe from the whole scenario, and started thinking about next steps, the most imperative of which was that I needed information: how big was the warehouse, where was it located, what was the security guard's schedule, how many cameras were there, and so on.

I took a deep breath. Yes, I was going all in. "Send me the specs. I'll get my team together," I wrote back. I imagined them at the other end of the conversation, giving each other quiet high fives and saying, "It's on. Player One is getting her team together. Send the file with the blueprints." While I waited for what I assumed would be a VERY appreciative response, I realized that I hadn't even asked about pay, like how many bundles of Bordens I was going to get (Bordens are the Canadian equivalent of Benjamins, but only 76 cents to the dollar). But while I was picturing a large leather case, and all those crisp Bordens, the reply came: "What do you mean?"

It suddenly occurred to me that, perhaps, I had badly misjudged the offer. I wrote back, "Is this a job, or a 'job'?" Again, the answer came back: "What?" I did the only thing I could do, and replied, "Wrong number."

Driving Heavy Machinery

What is it about me that I regularly get job offers via text random text message? The next time my text notification went off, I sighed and braced myself for more warehouse shenanigans but it was something much better, potentially a dream come true. I have regularly waxed poetic on a number of occasions about driving a forklift. And why WOULDN'T I want to drive one? A forklift is like a golf cart with arms, and if you know anything about me, you should know that the only reason I have EVER golfed is so I can drive the golf cart, and a forklift is just one step better. It's like being a human transformer. If you've ever seen that Alien movie where Sigourney Weaver wears the forklift suit, you'll know what I'm talking about. The only thing more badass than a forklift suit is in the final installment of The Matrix where Captain Mifune wears the human machine gun suit. They call it an 'Armoured Personnel Unit', but if it was me, I'd just be yelling "Get me my goddamned human machine gun suit—Player One's got a dock to defend!!"

And what did this magical text message say? It said, "Urgent Requirements! Forklift Operators needed! Long hours and long term possible. Text TPI!" and there was a number to text back. There was also the sentence "Text STOP to opt out", but in this case, I would NEVER want to opt out. I was momentarily thrilled and was about to text back, "Yes! A resounding yes!" when I read it again. Long hours? Long term possible? That didn't sound like much fun to me. I mean, 45 minutes would be good—that would give me a chance to tool around the neighbourhood, go to the park and rearrange some picnic tables, you know, the normal sh*t you do with a forklift (in this scenario, I'm obviously wearing a cape and a Spanish Inquisitor hat because no one expects the Spanish Inquisition, particularly on a forklift). But anything longer than that might become more like a job than a pleasure, and I already had a job.

So I texted back, "Ooh, I've always wanted to drive a forklift. But I don't think I could do it for hours, more just like around the block or whatnot. Thanks though!" That was the end of it, and I was a little sad, thinking I would never hear from them again, but about ten minutes later, my text notification went off again. I didn't look right away, assuming it was Jim Gaffigan talking about manatees AGAIN, but no—it was from the forklift people. The text read, "Thank you!" So now I don't know if that means they're considering me and one day this week a forklift might pull into my driveway, but I have my cape and hat ready to go.

But I have obsessed very often about driving a forklift, and then I went one step further when I had to have an MRI and my surgeon asked if I had any metal in my body. I didn't think so, but it occurred to me that if I DID, the metal I would want would be forklift arms, like what if my arms could transform into forklift arms or something, like Wolverine, you know? I'd be walking down the street and hear a cry for help and see an old lady (well, older than me anyway) lying trapped beneath a stack of wooden pallets that had just fallen on her, and my forklift arms would shoot out and rescue her by removing the pallets one by one. It would be a slow rescue, but it still counts.

And then Kate just read that over my shoulder:

Kate: Forklift arms? That's a terrible power. Go to Professor X with that, and he'd show you the door.
Me: No, he wouldn't. It's just as good as Wolverine, I mean what's his power? Spikes shoot out of his hands? You can't lift sh*t with those.
Kate: He's also immortal. And you don't need forklift arms to lift stuff when you HAVE ARMS.

But I still want forklift arms, despite the mockery. And of course, the other big question everyone asks when you tell them you're having an MRI is "Are you claustrophobic?" I started to get worried because from what I understood, the MRI machine is a giant magnet that they stick you in. That night, I woke up around 3 am as per usual, and lay there thinking about it, and when I imagined myself in a tight cave, I did get a little panicky. But then I googled pictures of MRI machines and they look more like very thick donuts, and you lie in the hole. So as long as I could get out either end, I'd be fine. Then the best part, and I'm being completely sarcastic here, is that they called and my appointment was for midnight. Midnight? I didn't have to worry about feeling claustrophobic—I'd be asleep. Unless the giant magnet triggered a hitherto unknown genetic mutation involving forklift arms...

Being A Spy

Once I was moving some stuff off an antique bench outside our bedroom, then when I went to shift the rest of the stuff ('stuff' is a great word—so non-specific and leaving things up to the reader's imagination and whatnot, but it was only magazines. Sorry to disappoint). I did this, finishing with a great flourish because I was pretending that I was in a swashbuckler movie as one does, when a very large splinter of wood jammed itself underneath the fingernail of my middle finger. I started squealing and saying "Ow! Ow!" because Ken was on his way out to get Kate from a friend's house, and I wanted him to know I was in pain. I hadn't looked at the splinter yet, but I suspected it was pretty far down my fingernail. Ken started yelling from downstairs "What? What did you do? Where are you?!" and eventually we met in the middle.

I showed him my finger (which I still hadn't looked at) and first he said, "Why are you giving me the finger?", and then he said, "Holy sh*t! How did you manage that?" like, somehow, my actual intention had been to stab myself. Also, his shocked expression told me that

WHAT ANY NORMAL PERSON WOULD DO

MAYBE the splinter was quite a bit bigger than I thought, plus it was really starting to hurt. "Fix it, Fix it!" I said to him, and he looked at it for a minute in that way he has, where he's deciding what power tool might be best for the job at hand (no pun intended). Eventually, with me continuing to make unhappy noises and jumping up and down a little, he said, "Come with me—I have tweezers in the bathroom." But first he had to clip my nail all the way down, then surgically extract the wooden dagger, which hurt as much coming out as it did going in. After the whole ordeal was over, he gave me a big hug and kissed my head, which was very sweet, and then we decided (or at least I did, with Ken indulging me) that I could be a spy for sure, because if the enemy tried to get any information out of me by jamming splinters underneath my fingernails, I wouldn't give away any secrets.

Me: See, you could have asked me anything, and I wouldn't have told you. It wasn't that bad.
Ken: Sure, honey. But I think the bamboo splinters that torturers use are a bit longer.
Me: You'll never know what I'm going to get you for next Christmas. You could have tried asking me when I had the splinter in my finger, but I wouldn't have said anything.
Ken: Yep, you were a real trooper.

I'm pretty sure he was being sincere and not sarcastic. I really would make a great spy, unless the enemy dangled me off a balcony. For more on this see **Chapter 3: Queen Of Worst -Case Scenarios**.

Let's Face It—I'd Be Good At All The Jobs

I've been on LinkedIn for about several years now. If you don't know what LinkedIn is, it's like Facebook for people who don't want to read about your vacation, see pictures of your kids, or look at memes about cats. Anyway, the purpose of LinkedIn is to let you network with other "professionals", post interesting "professional" articles, and read about "professional"-type things. Frankly, it's boring AF for someone like me, who only dabbles in "professionalism" and would actually prefer to read about your vacation or see pictures of your kids than learn about how I can "benefit from a global logistical hub connecting people, goods and markets through sky and sea".

Last year though, I was looking through my account and found a button I could activate that would tell people I was 'on the market', i.e. looking for a job. I wasn't actually looking for a job, since I already had a couple, but still, I thought, "I'm retiring soon. What's the harm in seeing what's on offer?" It's the same logic as being in a happy marriage, but looking over your friend's shoulder while she's swiping left and right on Tinder—it's fun to see what's out there, even if you're not really interested at the moment. So I signed up (for Job Alerts, NOT Tinder). But then, at least three times a day, I would get a LinkedIn Job Alert that showed me over 100 jobs for which I might, apparently, be a 'top applicant'. And also, apparently, LinkedIn has no idea what I did for a living, or what my current skill sets were because I didn't even know what some of these jobs entailed. But what if I applied for one and actually got it?...

Supervisor, Tool Room

Me: Good morning, staff. I am your new Supervisor, Tool Room.

Staff (muttering—they're a cynical bunch apparently): Yeah, good morning, whatevs.

Me: So, first things first. Please put your tools on the table so that I can supervise them. I've devised this clever sign-out system, so if you need a tool, I've also created a Word document explaining how you fill in the requisition form. There will be a quiz tomorrow. Have a good day.

Staff: What the f*ck? Give us back our hammers!

Warehouse Support

Me: You are an excellent warehouse. Don't feel bad because you aren't always as creative as the other warehouses. Creativity comes in many forms. We just have to find the right…idiom for you.

Warehouse: I just really want to get better at abstraction. I mean, my realistic canvases are quite well-received, but I want to branch out—you know, show the other warehouses that there's more to me than just landscapes.

Me: You will. Trust me.

Team Leader, Change Implementation

Me: Good morning, staff. I'm your new Team Leader. My job is to implement change.

Staff (enthusiastically—these guys are much more receptive): Okay, cool, whatevs.

Me: As of today, you are no longer "Waterloo-Wellington Agricorp Limited, Finance and Procurement Division". You are now "Frosty Queen". Let's hear it for frozen milk products!

Staff: But we make farm equipment.

Me: Change is hard.

Security Shift Supervisor

Me: Good morning team. I understand that you are the Security Shift. I like it. That's an awesome nickname. So which one of you is Deadpool, because I just LOVE how you combine humour with kick-ass action.

Staff (confused—not the sharpest tools in the shed I'm also supervising): Deadpool? What are you talking about?

Me: Oh. Is this more of a Suicide Squad-type deal? OK. Which one of you is Harley Quinn?

Girl (slowly raises hand).

Me: Cool. I didn't recognize you out of costume.

Girl: Uh, no. There's no 'Harley Quinn' here.

Me: Then which universe IS this?! I get them so confused, especially since Marvel AND DC are both putting teasers after the credits. All right, "Security Shift"—show me your superpowers. And do it quick—I hear there's trouble down at the Frosty Queen.

Bilingual French Financial Services Funding Specialist

Me (terrible French accent): Doo yoo wahnt sum mun-ayyy?

French Person: Je ne comprend pas!

Me: Mun-ayyy! Le cash! Do you actually SPEAK French or are you just messing with me?

French Person: Vous etes une idiote.

Me: Aww. That's sweet. But you forgot the accent circonflexe on 'etes'. (My written French is MUCH better than my spoken French).

Advanced Case Manager, Insurance Products

Me: So a shark attacked your boat and it sunk?

Customer: Aye. We're gonna need a bigger boat.

Me: Unfortunately, you're only insured for the replacement cost. Also, shark attacks are an act of God.

Customer (scratches nails down the blackboard that I somehow have in my fancy insurance office): Argh. You suck.

Me: I'm sorry, Mr. Quinn. I CAN, however, provide some funds for the purchase of extra scuba tanks and a rifle.

Customer: I can't see how that would be helpful, but whatevs.

Broadband Specialist

Me: I hear the internet is slow. Where do we keep the extra wire-y type things?

Staff: In the warehouse. Be careful when you go in—it has self-esteem issues.

As you can see, I would be amazing at so many of the jobs that LinkedIn was offering me. But now that I'm actually retired, the job postings are coming in hot and heavy, and they just keep getting more bizarre. First, there was a faculty position to teach *Introduction To Neuropsychology*, but I think to take a job like that, you need to know what neuropsychology is aside from 'weird brain stuff'. There WAS an intriguing post for 'Collections Specialist' and I was thrilled for a minute because, as you know, I collect a LOT of things, but it was actually just a euphemism for shaking down people over the phone to get them to pay their debts, and I've never seen the word 'delinquent' used so much in one ad. Ultimately, I think I need to give up on these sites, because I never know what the jobs are, and I spent a lot of time the other day coming up with various configurations of meats, cheeses, and condiments to demonstrate my creativity, only to discover that "Sub Stack Developer" was not quite what I imagined it to be.

But I'm not a quitter, so I've decided to use my entrepreneurial spirit and come up with my own jobs, positions that are a LOT more fun than "Mobile Truck and Coach Technician" or "Procurement

Operations Specialist" (which is code for professional kidnapper, obviously):

Travel Advisor

This is not the same thing as a travel agent. No, what I'll be doing is using my extensive experience as Queen of Worst Case Scenarios to help people who are thinking of travelling:

Client: So I'd like to go hiking.
Me: Terrible idea.
Client: But I really want to go.
Me: Fine. Don't stand on the edge of any cliffs.
Client: Ooh, good thinking.
Me: And don't clamber around on rocks. Your ankle could get caught in between two of them, and then you'd have to chew your leg off. Also, get some bear spray.
Client: Excellent advising. Here is fifty dollars.

Boredom Specialist

Me: I see that you are the Synergy Group, Boring Division. I'm here to help you spice things up.
Guy working on my street: That's not what that means.
Me: So your division isn't boring?
Guy: Well, yes. It IS boring, but--
Me: Then you definitely need my help. I suggest a clown costume,

the bigger and redder the nose the better. Also, two words—glitter cannon.

Guy: Lady, leave me alone. I need to do boring.

Me: Fine. Be boring. But don't say I didn't try. And on that note, you owe me fifty bucks.

Pet Detective

I actually saw that job title come up the other day, and I was super excited at the idea of combining two of my favourite things—solving mysteries and pets. And this was even better because it was solving mysteries ABOUT pets. The position involved 'striking up conversations and sharing stories with fellow pet owners about their animals' and it sounded EXACTLY like what a good detective would do:

Me (striking up conversation): Hello. Might I ask you a couple of questions?

Pet Owner: Why certainly.

Me (holds up photograph): Have you seen this cat anywhere? Her name is Miss Whiskers McGee. She was last seen in the company of your bulldog.

Bulldog (running): You'll never take me alive!

Pet Owner: Bowzer! What have you done?!

And I had just gone through the closet and found one of Ken's old fedoras and a trenchcoat when Ken pointed out that the job was with the Blue Buffalo Pet Food Company and that 'Pet Detective' was a glorified pet food salesperson and I was like "How in the name of Nancy Drew is that doing detective work?!" But then the other day, our neighbour's cat escaped from their breezeway and they asked us to help find her. We didn't--she was hiding in their basement ceiling--but if it happens again, I'm definitely wearing the fedora and trenchcoat.

Also I Excel At STEM

STEM, if you didn't know this, stands for Science, Technology, Engineering, and Math. There's a lot of concern about getting more girls into STEM fields and rightly so. But recently, I realized that I've become very STEM-y as I've aged:

Science:

Up until a little while ago, I really struggled with directions. Not directions like "Twist off cap and pour", but the actual compass directions. If somebody told me to go North, I would just look at them blankly and be like, "Which way am I NOW? Is North left, right, up or down from here?" But then I realized that I shouldn't take pride in being perpetually one step away from being lost in the woods, so I decided to become better at navigation. It's easy in the big city, where Yonge Street acts as a permanent point of reference: towards the lake is South and the other way is North. Then I can just mentally orient myself from there. I've also been working on this at home based on which way our house faces. It's West, by the way. We've lived here for eighteen years, and I just found that out five years ago. I'm a work in progress.

I'm also very good at telling the difference between real science and pseudo-science. Many years ago, Ken and I lived in a different house with a well that kept going dry. A neighbour suggested that we get a water witch to come out. Apparently, this witch—well, warlock really—had a great reputation at locating the ideal spot for a new well. So he came to the house with his dousing rods, wandered about for a bit waving them around, and then said, "There's so much water on this land!" He said this while standing next to a 12-foot-deep pond, and 100 yards away from the Otter Creek. Thanks, Merlin.

Technology:

Once, when Ken was away, the bathroom faucet broke. I called a plumber who told me that a service call was $160 just to look at it, then $160 for every hour after that to fix it. I was appalled, and also a little disappointed that I hadn't gone into the skilled trades. My mom asked, "What are you going to do?" And I said, "Imma fix it my damned self." That's a direct quote. I don't know why I phrased it like that, but in retrospect, it was a tad overconfident.

I watched a couple of YouTube videos, through which I learned that the first thing you have to do is turn off the water. So I got back from work, and pulled out the pot drawer (actual pots, not marijuana, just so we're clear), and I looked for the shut-off. Then I did what any normal person would do. I called Ken.

Me: I just sent you a picture of the underneath of the sink. Which way do I turn the knob?

Ken: Are you sure that's the right one? It looks like it goes to the dishwasher.

Me (crawling inside the cupboard): Oh yeah. The pipes come in from the bathroom. Hang on a minute.

5 minutes later…

Me: I took the drawer out of the vanity and I see the taps. I sent you a picture.

Ken: The valves are right there. Turn them to the right.

Me (crawling inside vanity): They won't move. They're stuck.

Ken: Do you know where the WD-40 is?

Me (pleasantly surprised): Why yes. Yes I do.

To make a long story short, after about half an hour and half a can of WD-40, the shut off valves moved and I turned off the water. I used an Allen key to remove the faucet handle, and I could see the set screw. I was almost at the cartridge thing-y that the guy on YouTube said was the problem. But then, the stupid set screw stripped as I was trying to take it out with my rather suspect "universal screwdriver". I ended up having to put the whole thing back together, all angry and sweaty from being inside very small cabinets; otherwise we would have had no water at all. Eventually, Ken came home and fixed it himself. But at least I tried.

Engineering:

No one knows what Engineers do. I probably do a lot of Engineering type things without even realizing it, and I'm most likely VERY good at them.

Math:

I know I already spent a very large portion of the previous chapter (at least 60%) talking about how I suck at math, but hear me out. Five years ago, Ken built a new porch for the front of our house. It was an exciting project, and every day he got a little bit more accomplished. I was helping out where I could, passing screws, holding a piece of wood straight or whatnot, but it was getting harder because then he started asking me math questions.

> **Ken:** I need to build three more steps. They're five feet wide with a run of 17 inches between them. How many linear feet do you think I need?
>
> **Me:** How fast are the trains going and what time did they leave the station…?
>
> **Ken:** I need to buy wood for the steps. I'm thinking of 2x8s.
>
> **Me:** But if the steps are 17 inches deep, then that's only 16. Don't you want them to hang over a little? What about getting 2x6s and using three per step?
>
> **Ken:** Ooh, you're doing grown-up math!

Me: F*ck off.

People tease me about not being proficient with math, and I make fun of myself all the time too, but the fact is that I'm actually very mathematical when I put my mind to it. For example, I know based on scientific calculations that my favourite wine glass will hold five ounces of wine if I fill it to a certain level, and thanks to careful research (Google) with white wine at 120 calories per five-ounce serving size, I know exactly how much I can drink every day. I hope you're impressed because I'm just f*cking dazzling myself with my math/wine prowess. Also, last year, I had to write my mom a cheque for the deposit on a cruise I was taking with her and my dad, as well as the money for my brother's birthday present. And as a math prodigy, I used the tools at hand to make the calculations. And I mean LITERALLY at hand, because I wrote the numbers ON MY HAND and added them up.

Fixing Stuff:

Like a lot of people, I'm pretty good at MacGyvering—that is to say that I can solve complicated household problems with very common household items. I come by this skill honestly—my father was a machine shop teacher and toolmaker by trade. He can make a tool to fix just about anything out of an Allen key, and there were always several things in our house held together with contact cement. Me, I prefer Gorilla Glue, but same concept. Last month, the gingerbreading on our Victorian screen door broke, and there was no way to screw or nail it back together, so I just glued it. Worked like a sticky charm. I have my own utility drawer in the kitchen which contains the only 4 actual tools I've ever needed. 1) One of the many hammers I own 2) needle nose pliers 3) a multi-screwdriver 4) a staple gun.

Everything else is assorted flotsam that I can use to MacGyver, including:

a) Cardboard: This is handy for folding up and putting under a table leg or whatnot to stabilize it. Also, our house is very old and tilty, so sometimes cupboard doors will just swing open. There's nothing like a cardboard wedge to keep them in place. Neatly hidden of course—who wants to see cardboard?

b) Plastic food containers: I recently put the empty tub from a very delicious garlic spread upside down in a large plant pot in order to raise my Thanksgiving chrysanthemum up high enough that it could be seen. I could have used a smaller plant pot, but hey—I had an empty tub and why waste it?

c) Paper clips: These are a multi-use invention that I have rarely used on paper. Zipper pull on your boot broken? Paper clip. Screen on your hair dryer clogged? Paper clip. Feel like poking a hole in something? Paper clip. Bored at work? Paper clip. Enough said.

d) Toothpicks: These handy little gadgets are terrific for repairing reading glasses. One leg is ALWAYS going to fall off and the screw is going to disappear into a space/time void. What better item to use to fix it than a toothpick? Just shove one through the screw holes and snap it off. No one will ever know. Also, if you have 17 jar candles that are burned down really far, and trying to light them with a match burns your fingers, make a longer match with a bunch of toothpicks taped together.

e) You can hang a picture on a pushpin if it's not too heavy. You can move any piece of furniture across a smooth surface by putting a towel under it and dragging it. You can wrap duct tape around your hand, sticky side out, and use it as a clothes lint remover. SOS pads are the only thing I use to clean old, dirty wood before I refinish it.

And so on. But a few years ago, when I was living in Toronto during the week for work, I had my most MacGyver-y challenge yet. My most recent roommate, who was a vegan, messaged me to tell me that she had broken her toilet. "I went to see the concierge," she wrote, "but he said you would have to hire a private contractor."

"What part of the toilet is broken?" I asked. She sent a picture of the chain.

Private contractor? Hah! I thought to myself, putting three paper clips into my purse to take back to the condo. "Don't worry," I told her. "I'll take care of it."

Now, the only thing the girl ate was fruit, so I don't know WHY she was flushing the toilet hard enough to break the chain, but

I don't eat a lot of roughage either and I recently broke a toilet in the train station. I didn't tell the station attendant, who is always extremely rude to me—I just got off the train and fled, leaving behind a complete f*cking disaster that I refer to as "her karma". So who am I to judge?

At any rate, I got back to the condo, went straight to my roommate's bathroom and examined the toilet. I drained it first, then I pulled out the chain. Turns out it wasn't the chain itself that had broken—the thing on the flapper that the chain was attached to had been ripped off. Well, the flapper was rubber and I had a paper clip, which is always handy for poking holes into stuff. All I needed to do was pierce the flapper with the paper clip and then attach the paper clip to the chain.

Unfortunately, the rubber was too thick and all I managed to do was pierce my own thumb. Once I was finished swearing, I thought for a minute, and went to my utility drawer. Eureka! I had a push pin. A yellow push pin to be exact. I pushed it into the rubber flapper without sympathy (revenge for my thumb) and hooked a paper clip around it, which I then twisted around the chain. I filled the tank back up and gave it a flush. Perfect. "Flush away!" I told her. "It's all fixed."

The next morning, I was at work when I got another text message. "I'm so sorry," it read. "I must have flushed too hard—the chain came off again." Then I remembered that she had had a large meal of pumpkin and pineapple the night before—perhaps that was the culprit. Then came the second message: "And the pushpin went down the pipe." I felt more than a little defeated at the thought that all my MacGyvering had amounted to nothing. It was time to watch

YouTube videos and buy actual parts. Which I did after work. I bought three different flappers, not knowing which one would work the best. Luckily, the first one seemed to do the trick, so after draining the toilet, installing it, and practicing a few good flushes, it seemed good as new. "Just be gentle with it," I made her promise. "And you owe me a new pushpin."

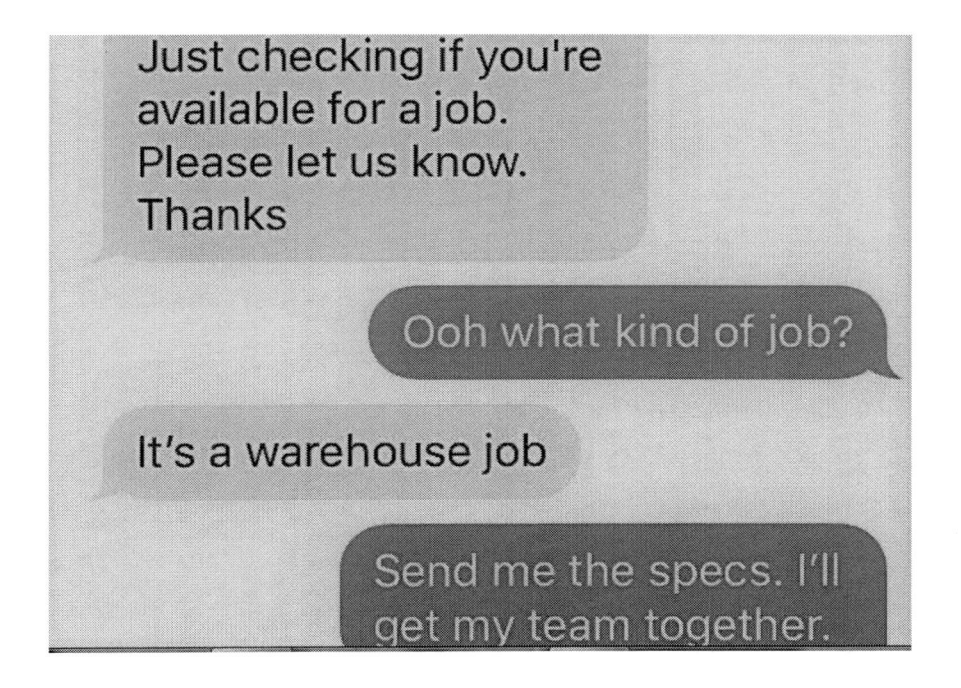

> Just checking if you're available for a job. Please let us know. Thanks

>> Ooh what kind of job?

> It's a warehouse job

>> Send me the specs. I'll get my team together.

CHAPTER 3: QUEEN OF WORST-CASE SCENARIOS

So I was talking to Ken on the phone the other morning, and as we were saying goodbye, his parting comment was, "It's really windy out. Be careful." And he said it kind of ominously. But this was the completely wrong thing to say to me, because anyone who knows me understands that I go immediately into Queen of Worst-Case Scenario mode any time someone tells me to be careful. So when Ken said that to me, my first response was confusion, then my mind immediately jumped to one of two scenarios: a) either he meant that it was so windy that I would need something heavy to hold me down so I wouldn't be whisked away by a howling gale, in which case I seriously started looking around the house for something heavy to take with me. The dog weighs 95 pounds, but I would have to be tethered to him by his leash, and could I hold on for long enough? Or b) that the wind was some kind of bizarre polar vortex, and if I didn't run fast enough to the car, I would freeze on the spot, like the characters did in *The Day After Tomorrow*, which is a great movie, and totally based on meteorological facts.

At any rate, when I had recovered from my frightful befuddlement, I asked him, "Why are you telling me to be careful? That's just weird", and he was like, "Because you never dress warmly enough, so make sure you wear a scarf, okay?" At which point, I really felt like saying, "Are you f*cking serious? You freaked me out over a scarf?! There's NOTHING in the *Little Book of Worst-Case Scenarios* about scarves." But then it occurred to me that a scarf might be the only thing standing between me and deathly hypothermia, and I realized that Ken must really love me to give me scarf warnings.

The main thing about being the Queen of Worst-Case Scenarios is that you always have to think ahead and plan for the worst. I've literally spent a great portion of my life creating plans to survive things like falling out of airplanes, being attacked by sharks, drowning, tornadoes, floods, falling through ice, and a myriad of other perceived (and not very likely to occur) dangers.

Is it stressful? Incredibly. I'm regularly wracked with anxiety by thinking of all the Worst-Case Scenarios that might occur in any given situation and how to manage them. For example, travelling. Five years ago, Ken and I decided to go on a complicated vacation, flying first to Calgary, then driving to Edmonton, followed by getting on a train to Vancouver. Finally, we would be taking a ship to Alaska. The whole 'adventure' kicked my obsessive need to plan for the worst into high gear. I'd already figured out how to survive a train derailment when we were in Spain, and the lifeboat drills on a cruise ship are a tremendous comfort to me. I knew I couldn't do anything about the plane unless it landed in water but I booked an aisle seat just in case. (Ken: You should wear running shoes on the plane in case it crashes and we have to go down the slide. Me: I'm wearing flip flops in case we're in water and I have to use them like flippers.)

But there are other forces outside of my control that make travelling very stressful for me; for example, finding out three weeks before the trip that the train would be arriving in Vancouver 9 hours late. It hadn't even left the damn station yet--how did they know?! The best I could do was build a 24-hour buffer into each of these segments of our journey because anyone who knows me well, knows that I always plan ahead. In fact, when Kate was very small, I bought her *The Little Book of Worst-Case Scenarios* so that even she, as a young child, could start to plan for disasters such as:

a) Bear Attacks: Make yourself look as large as possible and scream loudly to let the bear know you could take it in a fight. Do not run—bears are, apparently, very gazelle-like—unless you're with someone who runs slower than you.

b) Driving a car into a river: Find an air pocket, wait for the car to be submerged, then open the door and swim to the surface. (Kate was like "I'm seven years old--why would I ever drive my car into a river?" I DON"T KNOW, KATE. But if you plan for these things, you might SURVIVE them, and now that you're an adult and have a driver's license, it's a damn good thing you know about this).

c) Bouncy Castle Mishaps: The survival rate for a bouncy castle you're playing in which suddenly becomes untethered and floats away (which apparently happens more often than you think) is very poor.

That's why my child had boring but safe birthday parties.

So after years of careful consideration and planning, I feel ready for almost anything, like wrestling an alligator or even escaping from a burning bus. For example, I have hammers in strategic places around the house, which prompted Ken to ask, "Why do you have a hammer in the bathroom?" Answer: in case there's a fire, and I can't get to my new fire extinguisher, and I have to smash the bathroom window and crawl out onto the porch roof. Obviously. Here's another example--in the winter, we put a wheelbarrow over the pond in our backyard so that our dog doesn't fall through the snow into the frigid water. This happened to our previous dog, prompting a very heated argument which had followed this earlier argument:

Ken: I'm going to dig a 3-foot-deep pond.
Me: Don't be ridiculous. Someone will fall in and drown.
Ken: No one is going to fall in. You're worrying for no reason. It needs to be deep so the fish can survive the winter.
Me: I'm serious. Please, I'm begging you, don't make it so deep.
Ken: I'm totally disregarding your emotions and I'm going to do what I want. Screw you. (OK, he didn't actually say any of THAT, but he DID continue to dig a 3-foot-deep pond despite my objections).

6 months later, we let the dogs out into the back yard. The pond was covered by a healthy layer of snow, and about ten minutes later, we realized that we couldn't see one of the dogs, the really old one with bad arthritis. Yes, she had fallen into the pond, and it was

too deep for her to climb out. Ken rushed outside and rescued her, prompting this heated argument, which I will sum up in one sentence:

> **Me:** OMFG!! I TOLD you this would happen!! And the fish are all DEAD!!
>
> Hence the wheelbarrow which straddles the pond all winter.

I also have a baseball bat under my side of the bed. And why do I keep a baseball bat under the bed? For the exact same reason I keep a hammer in the drawer of the bedside table. I also have both a hammer and a baseball bat in the bathroom, and a hammer in the family room, as well as two large oars in my office. I don't have either a hammer or a baseball bat in the kitchen because in the kitchen THERE ARE KNIVES. And all this is because I am the Queen of Worst-Case Scenarios. This is the scenario for the baseball bat:

1) We wake up in the middle of the night to strange noises coming from downstairs.

2) Ken, as one does, offers to investigate. He puts on his housecoat and goes down with the dog, who is clearly agitated.

3) I wait, wracked with fear. There are shouts, commotion, then nothing.

4) I assume that the intruder has tied both Ken and the dog up, and is taunting them as he steals our stuff.

5) I quietly get the baseball bat out from under the bed and sneak

downstairs. The intruder has his back to me.

6) Ken sees me, but luckily, he's gagged so he can't do what he would normally do and say something like, "Why do you have a baseball bat?!"

7) I swing, connect with the intruder's head, and down he goes.

8) I free Ken and our dog, we tie up and gag the intruder, and then we call the police. Ta dah!

Would it happen like this in real life? Hopefully we'll never have to find out.

So you see, I have impending disasters carefully planned, even when I lived in Toronto where I rented a condo during the week in a high rise building on the 34th floor. This, of course, led to a whole new set of Worst-Case Scenarios. For example, I had a balcony. Everyone is always like, "Awesome, you have a balcony—I'll bet you can't wait until it's nice enough to sit out there." Are you f*cking kidding me? Do you think there's ANY way I would EVER sit out on a precipice that is over 400 feet from the ground? And here's why. It occurred to me that balconies figures prominently in several Worst-Case Scenarios, which I am slowly working my way through. Here's the one I solved during my first month there, as I lay awake listening to the baby next door screaming like it was being throttled (it wasn't, of course; when I politely inquired after its health in the morning, the mother told me they were "sleep training" him, and he was "very unhappy" about it. Oh yeah? I'll bet he wasn't as unhappy as me.)

Anyway, I suddenly had this horrible thought that, say, I did take someone's advice and try to grow pots of basil on the balcony. I go out on the balcony to water my plants, and somehow the door closes and locks behind me. I don't know how that would actually happen, but say that it did. What now? I'm stuck on a 34th floor balcony, wearing only pajamas (because that's what I was wearing when I started trying to solve this problem).

Option A: Scream for help. No, because I'm 34 floors up. No one on the ground can hear me, and the neighbours' eardrums have been damaged by their 'unhappy' child.

Option B: Take off an article of clothing to wave around and attract attention. Well, I'm only wearing pajama bottoms and a T-shirt—which one do I use? I guess I have to decide HOW MUCH attention I actually want. But who will see me that high up anyway?

Option C: Start tossing the basil pots down to the ground until someone looks up and sees me (either topless or pantless) and calls the cops. This solution is unlikely because my experience with people downtown has been that many of them are either completely self-absorbed and oblivious to the world around them, or looking down at the ground for cigarette butts.

No, the only sure thing is **Option D:** Keep an extra hammer out on the balcony. Then I can smash the glass in the patio door and get back into my condo. The hammer people must love me. Not only do

I have several scattered around my house, I purchased two for Toronto as well.

(Fun fact: Via Trains are equipped with tiny hammers in boxes to smash the windows in case people get somehow trapped in the train. Nice to know they've been paying attention.

> **Car Attendant to our train car:** So you all know what to do in case of emergency?
> **Me:** Absolutely. I call out "Mjolnir", the hammer inside the box flies into my hand, I use it to break the window, and I lead everyone to safety.
> **Car Attendant:** Uh…
> **Other People:** *stare in confusion*
> **Me:** The hammer won't come if I call it?
> **Car Attendant (laughs):** No, but I enjoyed the Thor reference, ma'am.
> **Me:** Please—just call me Player One.)

And of course, as the Queen Of Worst-Case Scenarios, I naturally have a fire extinguisher in the kitchen. Not because I may or may not have almost set the kitchen on fire three times whilst making brandy peppercorn sauce until I learned to add the brandy once the butter and onions had cooled down instead of pouring it into the frypan on high heat with a remarkably sophisticated flourish, but because Ken is a daredevil and I need to save him from himself…

One spring, I had to put the fireplace on because this is Canada, and the weather can be minus 5 one day, and 30 degrees (38 with the humidex) the next. We literally had a heat wave one March from Monday to Friday, then on Saturday morning, it was 8 degrees Celsius (about 45 Fahrenheit for people who don't have to worry about everything being in fancy wizard math), and I was wearing a sweatshirt instead of sweating.

His work for the moment finished, Ken announced that he was walking to the corner to get gas for the lawnmower that he had been trying to fix for 6 weeks. While he was gone, I was in the back room talking to the dog about whether or not he was a good boy, as one does:

Me: You're so sweet. Who's a good boy?
The dog: Is that rhetorical? Because obviously me.
Me: That's right. You ARE a good boy. You're so snuggly.
The dog: Yeah, this snuggling is great. Wait—what was that?
Me: What?
The dog: That noise? Didn't you hear it?

Suddenly I heard this awful screeching sound. It was coming from the fireplace in the living room. I ran in and came around the corner just in time to see black smoke pouring out of the fan vents. Now, that might not be weird for a wood fireplace, but this one was gas. Naturally, I freaked out. I ran over, giving the front a wide berth in case it chose that moment to explode, turned the thermostat off so it would be less flame-y, then I did what any normal person would do—I started yelling for Ken.

Ken didn't answer. I ran up and down the sidewalk but there

was no response. I was terrified, but I went back in. It was still making the same deafening screeching noise and I could smell something burning, so I picked up the phone and called 9-1-1. I explained to the operator that I needed the fire department in a kind of staccato "Fireplace—smoke—gas—send help—" way, and she told me the fire department was coming and to get out of the house. I grabbed the dog, put him in the back yard, then ran to the front, phone in hand and tears running down my face, still looking for Ken. I found him chatting with the next-door-neighbours. I screamed, "There's something wrong with the fireplace. I called 9-1-1!" He came running (well, loping because Ken never runs, which makes him the perfect companion in bear territory) right past me and towards the house.

Me: What are you doing?! The 9-1-1 lady said NOT to go in!!
Ken: I'm going to turn off the breaker!
Me: You're not allowed to go in!
Ken: It's fine! It's probably just the motor!
Me: Don't go in! I order you to stay outside—
Ken: *disappears into the house*

Anyway, he turned off the breaker and the screeching stopped. There wasn't any more smoke, although the air still smelled charred, but there was no smell of gas, and that was a good sign. We stared at the fireplace for a minute. It seemed like it was no longer about to explode, so I tried cancelling the 9-1-1 call, but it was too late. The next thing, firetrucks were pulling up to the house and some very nice firefighters helped us check everything out. Apparently, there was a tag on a wire next to the fan, and when I was vacuuming out the dust the day before, the tag got dislodged and ended up in the fan blades, causing the fan to overheat. Embarrassing as it was, the firefighters were really great and they waited while we turned the fireplace back on to see what would happen. It came back on quietly, and all was good, so the fire department left.

And then the very next Friday, Ken did the following in this exact sequence:

1) Start a fire in the burn pit.

2) Fill up the lawnmower with gas.

3) Try to start the lawnmower.

4) Defend the lawnmower to his wife thusly: "It's not broken. It always takes this many pulls to start it."

5) Finally get the lawnmower started.

6) Begin mowing the lawn around the burn pit.

7) Ignore his wife's screams. Yell, "I can't hear you over the lawnmower! You're downwind!"

8) Push the gas lawnmower onto the flaming burn pit in an attempt to cut the grass around it as close as he can.

19) Be forced to turn the lawnmower off when screaming wife (see

number 7) stands in front of the mower to berate him.

Naturally, I was very unhappy:

Ken: What?!
Me: What the f*ck is wrong with you? You just filled the lawnmower up with gas! It could explode!
Ken: Why are you scolding me like I'm a five-year-old?
Me: Why are you mowing the lawn like you're a five-year-old?!
Ken: What? That doesn't make any sense.
Me: Don't mow the firepit!

Words to live by, am I right? Anyway, he finished mowing and at a certain point, I heard him trimming the edges of the flower beds with the weed whacker. After a while, the noise stopped so I went out to see if he wanted a drink. The weed whacker was lying in the exact middle of the patio and Ken was sitting on the deck staring at it with a mixture of bewilderment and dejection.

Me: What's wrong?
Ken: The weed whacker set on fire.
Me: What?!
Ken: Yeah. It started smoking and then flames literally shot out of it. I think we need a new one.
Me: Ya think?

So we went out and bought a fire extinguisher. It's small, so I can carry it with me everywhere. Just in case.

WHAT ANY NORMAL PERSON WOULD DO

The WORST-CASE SCENARIO® Little Book for Survival

HOW TO:
→ Escape from Quicksand
→ Wrestle an Alligator
→ Break Down a Door

CHAPTER 4: THE ANIMAL KINGDOM

One day, I was driving along and I saw a guy walking a dog. As I got closer, I realized that it was a dog with the body of a large Dachshund, and the face of a Rottweiler. It was a ROTTWIENER. And then I was really disappointed, because it didn't look bad-ass at all. You would think that a dog with the personality of a wiener dog, all scrappy and feisty, and the body of a Rottweiler, all muscular and mean, would be the height of bad-ass-ery. Nuh. It was just a bigger than average wiener dog with a round Rottweiler head. And it looked very awkward and self-conscious, like one of those dog-slinkies whose back end has a mind of its own. Why is it that the permutations of nature are never as cool as you hope they would be?

Then I got to thinking about other hybrid animals (because I was driving, so why not , right?) and it occurred to me that they all pretty much suck. For example, the mule. This is a cross between a horse and a donkey. Why would anyone WANT to do that? Especially the horse or the donkey? Who knows how it happens, except that apparently it's always a union between a donkey girl and a horse boy. Which makes sense because how would a boy donkey reach up that high? Then I thought the same must be true of the Rottwiener—it had to be a boy Rottweiler and a girl dachshund, or else SOMEONE was using a step stool.

Anyway, aside from the complicated logistics of these types of unions, the whole DNA component is also a puzzle. Why is it mules are sterile, but Rottwieners can go on to have little rotty-wiener babies, or even breed with another kind of dog, say, an Irish Wolfhound? Wouldn't that be a bizarre looking beast? I actually did a little research for this (i.e.: I googled "Crazy Animal Hybrids"), and while there were some real disappointments, like the Sheep-Goat (it's such a bad hybrid that it doesn't even get a cool name like Shroat, or Greep) I discovered some pretty amazing creatures, so here are my top 3:

3) The Liger

This is a cross between a lion and a tiger. It's the biggest cat known to humans and can be over 10 feet long and weigh 700 pounds. Also, its best friends are Heffalumps and Woozles.

2) The Grolar Bear

Created when a grizzly bear and a polar bear mate. While this seems unlikely, given that polar bears live NO WHERE NEAR grizzly bears, scientists speculate that it's happening more and more in the wild due to global warming, and grizzly bears moving into formerly polar bear-only areas. See, global warming has its upside, which is awesome new animals. As the earth warms up and other ecosystems change, maybe we'll also see the Pengotter (yes, this is an imaginary cross between a penguin and an otter, which I made up just now, and it would be the cutest thing to ever exist).

1) Coydog

The number one best animal cross, in my humble opinion, is the Coydog. According to the article I read, the Coydog has the natural cunning of a coyote without its instinctive fear of humans, making it tremendously high on the bad-ass scale. So it would pretend to be your best friend, and then when you were asleep, it would eat all your food and pee in your bed. Or kill you. And your Rottwiener.

Honourable Mention:

Of course, the Honourable Mention has to go to my favourite mythological hybrid animal—the Zebrasus. This is a cross between a zebra and a Pegasus. I have a sculpture of a Zebrasus on my shelf. I found it on a window ledge on the last day of school, many years ago, after all the students had gone home for the summer. I never found out who made it, but it was so awesome that I had to keep it for myself. The best thing about the Zebrasus, aside from the stripes and the wings, is that he's smoking a cigar. He is the Ultimate Bad-Ass.

Of course, most of those animals are not the ones you will usually encounter. So now, I will also rank the wild animals you might, on occasion, find in your house, from best to worst. I've had a lot of time, and a lot of animals, to consider this, and it occurs to me that other people might benefit from my experience of having a variety of wildlife in my house and cottage and which ones are better than others:

5) Bats

The best kind of animal to have in your house is a BAT. That sounds really crazy, but honestly, they aren't so bad. Bats have sonar, which is a fancy way of saying that they can tell where you are and won't fly into your face or hair, which is always a plus. Once, we were eating dinner, and Ken suddenly said, "A bat just flew by the doorway." I had my back to the kitchen at the time, so I said, "What?!" and turned around in time to see it fly past the doorway again. I ran into the corner with my dinnerplate, while Ken went to investigate, but he couldn't tell where it had gone. He also found it pretty amusing that I was freaked out but not enough to make me stop eating my dinner from the corner of our dining room. Well, I was hungry. At any rate, we searched the house, but it seemed to have disappeared, which was bad news, because I was NOT going to bed with a flappy bastard in the house. We had also just taken apart a piano, and I became irrationally convinced that the bat had been living in the piano, and I wouldn't go hear it for the rest of the night. Finally, around 11 o'clock, I went downstairs for one last glass of wine (wild animals always make me want to drink), when I saw it hanging quietly on a curtain. Ken came down, and cool dude that he is, he just wrapped it in a towel and let it out the door, while I drank wine and made squeamish sounds.

4) Mice

Mice are OK. We have mice once in a while. I don't mean that we have pet mice (well not up until now anyway); I mean that there are mice in our house. It's an old house with a partial basement and crawl space, and we hardly ever go down there because it's uber-creepy and the ceiling is so low that you have to walk hunched over. (Side note: There is an old cistern in the basement. Once, we had problems with our water softener, and a repair guy came to look at it. Out of the blue, he started telling me how the cistern had water in it, and I "should come down to the basement and take a look." I was alone in the house, so I was like, NO THANKS, but he kept insisting, until I had to lie and say a) I believed him so completely that seeing it for myself was unnecessary and that b) our dog at the time, a tremendously sweet yellow lab, was very protective and could be quite vicious if provoked. I said this while she stared at the dog cookie jar wagging her tail. He finally left, and I immediately locked all the doors.)

So anyway, every once in a while, there are mice. We know this because somehow they get into the cupboard under our sink, and leave poo everywhere. They can't get out into the actual house but it's still yucky and gross—apparently mice defecate continually, like little poo machines. We were using live traps for a long time, and Ken and I would drive the mice out to the country and let them go. I like to silently whisper "Fly, good Fleance, fly!" in an homage to Shakespeare's Macbeth and hope that the mouse understands that if it comes back, I might have to assassinate it to preserve my throne. I think I might be giving the mice too much credit, but they don't normally come back, so maybe my empty threats are working. But sometimes, the mice can be a little overwhelming, and have also figured out how to chew through the live traps. So Ken finally got fed up, and said to me in that domineering and commanding way he has, "I'm done with live traps. Get me the ones that KILL the mice, woman!" Okay, he didn't actually say "woman", but it makes for a great dramatic flourish, and he WAS rather commanding. I hated to do it, but I bought some traps, you know, those wooden ones that snap at you and make the horrible sound. Then last weekend, I woke up, and this was the conversation:

Ken: I caught a mouse last night, but the trap just got his leg. It's in Kate's room.
Me: I'm confused. The leg is…
Ken: The MOUSE is in Kate's room. She wouldn't let me kill it, so she got a lunch container, poked some holes in the lid, and the mouse is in it. His name is Jimmy.
Me: You named the mouse Jimmy?! What are we going to do with him?! What about his leg?
Ken: Kate named him. His leg is all right—it's just a bit funny-looking. We're taking him to the cottage with us.

I went into Kate's room, and there was Jimmy, looking quite lively despite the bum leg. Later that morning, we packed up, put Jimmy in the truck with us and the dog, who seemed absolutely unconcerned that a mouse was his travelling companion, and we drove to the lake. By this point, however, my maternal instincts had kicked in, and I started worrying about Jimmy. Were his air holes big enough?

Was he hungry or thirsty? Was he in pain? When we got to the cottage, I made him a wee water bowl out of a K-cup, and Kate and I researched the kind of food mice liked. We didn't have any of the things mice tend to eat (Kate had apparently been feeding him almond slices the night before, but we had no nuts at the cottage), so I gave him Rice Krispies, which he seemed more interested in tossing around than eating. Considering he'd been into our garbage until very recently, I thought it was kind of diva-ish of him, but I don't know mice very well.

Jimmy stayed on Kate's bedside table until the next morning, with all of us checking in on him regularly to make sure he was still happy. And alive. He was remarkably chipper, all things considered. That morning, after we finally got Kate out of bed, she and Ken took Jimmy outside to the composter (Ken was convinced that the middle of the compost pile would be warm and provide him with food) and by all reports (because I couldn't bear to see him go), when the container was opened, Jimmy hightailed it into the compost without so much as a backwards glance. "Live long and prosper, Jimmy," I whispered silently. But secretly, I hope he doesn't prosper too much, because I really don't want mice at the cottage. We've had enough trouble with squirrels.

Number 3: Rats

I became obsessed with rats after a colleague arrived at work one morning.

"God," she said. "As if the subway isn't gross enough, this

morning there was a HUGE rat running around on the tracks. Ugh."

And I was like, "A rat?! You saw a rat? Wow—I've never actually seen a real rat before." And then I got strangely jealous of my friend and her rat experience, and started feeling sad about it, like it was completely unfair that I never get to see rats. Now, if you've ever actually seen a rat yourself, you're probably thinking, "What the hell is wrong with you? You've seen squirrels, haven't you? They're essentially rats with bushy tails, so get over it." But no—squirrels aren't the same thing as rats. For one, nobody ever looks out their window and says, "Aww—look at all the cute rats scampering about the front yard. Ooh, that one's got some garbage!" I know that there are a lot of people who have pet rats, and from what I've seen from TV and the internet, they are pretty cute, but I'm talking hardcore, scavenging wild sewer rat here, the kind that people are referring to when they say "rat-infested". Don't get me wrong—I have absolutely no desire to have a colony of rats take up residence in my house or under my shed or whatnot. I know that actually happens to people and apparently, it's not very pleasant. I just want to see one with my own eyes, so when people say "Ugh—so gross!", I won't immediately think "Ratatouille" and be like "But they're so cute and charming...."

And it's weird that I've never seen a rat, because I've lived in the country for over 25 years, and I've yet to encounter one. Ken admitted to me a few years ago that one morning he was going down to the basement and saw a rat basking on one of the steps in the sunlight coming through the window. But before he could do anything (like call me down so I could SEE IT), the dog grabbed it and—well, things didn't bode well for "Sneaky Pete", which is exactly what I would have called him once he became my pet. I sometimes wish Ken hadn't told me about it, because it suddenly raised my hopes ("There was a rat on the basement steps this morning—") and then dashed them almost immediately ("—and the dog killed it."). As far as I know, there were never any more rats in the house, so now I will never be able to understand the saying, "I smell a rat" because I don't know what RATS SMELL LIKE.

Number 2: Raccoons

Raccoons are vicious beyond belief if they have babies. Once, I had a really bad cough so I was sleeping in our guest room. At one point during the night, I woke up to what sounded like an elephant moving furniture around in our attic. It was unbelievably loud and scary and possibly human, but the attic door locks from the inside-the-house side, so I figured that if it was a serial killer, he was pretty much stuck up there until Ken dealt with him, and I went back to sleep. In the morning, I told Ken about the noises, and he said he would investigate. I was taking a course at the time, so I told him I'd call him at the break and he could tell me what he found. When I called, Ken sounded a little distracted.

Me: Where are you right now?

Ken: In the attic.

Me: What did you find? Please tell me it's a rat—I mean, NOT a rat, obviously.

Ken: No…I'm staring right now at a very large mother raccoon and six newborn baby raccoons. She's kind of hissing at me.

Me: I'm going to say back away slowly. Don't break eye contact. If she goes for you, run.

Eventually, after several misadventures, and a lot of damage, including a hole chewed right through our roof (raccoons aren't the brightest apparently, and can't see their own offspring sleeping in a shoebox at the bottom of a TV tower), we caught her in a live trap. Ken had to carry her in the trap out of the attic, and through the house in order to get her outside. She was going insane, snarling and trying to attack the bars—I could tell Ken was a little intimidated by the way he was holding the trap as far away from his body as possible, and walking VERY quickly. We decided to take her and the babies down to the river flats where they could live happily ever after, but then we realized we had a major problem—what if, when we opened the cage, she tried to attack us in a fit of vengeful rage?

Ken had the great idea of using the cardboard box the live trap came in, putting it against the trap door, and letting her out into the cardboard box, which might disorient her long enough for us to jump back in the car and make a clean getaway. So we did that, but she somehow missed the cardboard box. I don't know what happened next because we were both already back in the car, having run for our lives. Ken went back later to get the trap, and both she and the babies were gone. I hope they had good lives down on the riverbank.

Number 1: Squirrels

The absolute worst thing to have in your house is a squirrel. Oh, but squirrels are so cute, you say. Yes, they are adorable, but NOT in your house. A couple of years ago, I got home from work, and was puttering around while Kate did her homework upstairs. I walked into our back family room, and as I passed the couch, I heard something sneeze. I looked around, and couldn't see the cat or dog anywhere, so I figured it was either my imagination or some weird old-house noise. But then when I came back the other way, I heard a sneeze again, and this time there was no doubt that it was coming from BEHIND THE COUCH. I just lost it—I ran upstairs, got Kate, and made her look behind the couch with a flashlight while I cowered around the corner in the kitchen.

Me: Can you see anything? Please tell me it's a rat—I mean NOT a rat, obviously.

Kate: I can't see anything yet—HOLY SHIT, there's something back there!!!!

Me: What?! What?!

Kate: I think it's an owl!

Me: An owl?! How the hell did an OWL get in our house?!

So I did what any normal person would do—I called Ken on his cell phone. He was about 5 minutes from home, and I made him stay on the line with me until he arrived, based on a bizarre belief that if he kept talking to me, the owl would leave me alone. Anyway, when he came in, he took a look and very calmly announced that it wasn't an owl, it was "only" a squirrel. This was a new experience for both of us, and while Ken pondered how best to get it out of the house, I poured a glass of wine and stayed on the other side of the room. Finally, he decided the best thing to do would be to open the door, push the couch away from the wall, and let the squirrel make a run for it. It did, but not after doing a couple of mad circuits around the room, trying to run up the wall, and falling back down (which I think stunned it a bit). Finally, it saw the open door, and took off. You'd think it would have been happy to escape and would have gone into hiding, but NO. It ran up a tree and spent the next ten minutes telling us exactly how pissed off it was that it had fallen down our chimney and ended up behind our couch, where apparently, it was very dusty. And while I thought I'd seen my last of Squirrel-y Dahmer, I had not.

Later that week, Ken called me to the window and said, "Look at that squirrel with a huge chunk of grass in its mouth. It's climbing up the downspout—what do you think it's doing?" and my response was "That little m*therf*cker!" because it was BUILDING A NEST under the decking of my balcony. So I went out and yelled "Hey!" and its head popped out, startled. We stared at each other, and in that moment, we both knew the game was on. I ran upstairs and out onto the balcony, which caused Squirrel-y Dahmer to scramble out and run to the corner of the roofline where he sat, staring at me like I was some bee that he was worried about, which then prompted me to point at him and yell, "I SEE YOU! Don't think for a minute that I don't know what the f*ck you're up to!!" because all I could keep thinking about was him popping up between the decking and biting my toes.

WHAT ANY NORMAL PERSON WOULD DO

After a few days of me randomly going out onto the balcony and stomping around, sending the dog out to intimidate him, and blasting heavy metal music at him, he eventually ran away, never to be seen again. Or DID he return?...

Because a month later, we were downstairs getting ready to go out, when Kate said, "Hey, do you hear that? It sounds like something is scratching inside the wall in the back room." So I listened, and sure enough, there was some kind of creature making a lot of noise, like it was trying to escape. But it wasn't coming from inside the wall—it was coming from inside an old chimney that has an access door into the top cupboard of a wall unit that Ken built. So we did what any normal person would do—we called Ken. Which is to say that Ken was taking a shower, so we both ran towards the bathroom, simultaneously yelling, "Ken!" and "Dad!" Ken came out of the shower, tied a towel around his waist, then went to the back room to look.

"Okay," he said. "I'm going to have to open the cupboard door." I immediately ran outside and locked myself behind the gate leading into the vegetable garden, and Kate hid behind the door to the backyard, where we taunted each other:

Me: Once that squirrel gets loose, it's going to eat your feet off.
Kate: No—it will eat YOUR face off.
Me: No—it'll hit the floor and go straight for your feet.
Kate: Haha—that's what you think—it'll go straight for the exit and fly at your face!
Ken (opening the door): I can't see anything—the squirrel must

have gone back up. But hey! The chimney is full of bird skeletons.

Me: Someone wake me up from this hellish nightmare.

You see, a couple of years ago, Ken had wrapped chicken wire around the top of the chimney to stop creatures from getting in, but apparently the wire had fallen down, and now it was a graveyard. Ken pulled all the dead stuff out and put it in a bag, but I was still worried and so for the rest of the day, we had to keep the door to the back room shut, because I was terrified that Squirrel-y Dahmer would climb back down the chimney, push his way out and kill us in our sleep. The only person who was happy about the whole situation was Ken:

Ken: Check this out!

Me: Why are you digging through all that dead sh*t?!

Ken: There are some awesome skulls in here! I can use them for a photography project.

Me: Are they maggoty? Stop digging in the bag—you're kicking up dead animal dust and I don't want it to get in my wine!

Ken: Ooh—this one is really nice. So clean! Oh look—a perfectly formed leg…

Me: I need more wine.

This, however, is not my only squirrel story. Let me introduce you to Squeaky Fromme, the cottage squirrel from hell. This entitled squirrel decided that she owned our summer place and she was super-intimidating. I started calling her "Squirrel Manson" until Ken pointed out that she had two rows of squirrel boobs, so I changed her name to "Squeaky Fromme". One day I looked up at the roof, and saw her halfway in and halfway out of a little hole under the eaves. I started screaming, and she took off. Later, Ken and I were sitting on the porch—I had my back to the driveway. Suddenly, I heard a noise, like a demon muttering, and I turned around—Squeaky was actually sneaking up on me. She had taken up residence in our attic, where she had some babies who were little serial-killer wannabes. We finally live-trapped them all and drove them out to the country (this, unfortunately, is not a euphemism—Ken was all like "Oh, we can't just kill them…" and normally I would agree, but that squirrel had devil-eyes).

Honourable Mention: Canada Goose

The evil lake chicken is known to Canadians far and wide as the most dangerous and unpredictable of the semi-wild animal kingdom. Once, I had a colleague who told everyone he quit smoking, then he snuck outside to have a cigarette. While he was puffing away, he looked up just as a Canada Goose swooped down and attacked him, knocking him to the ground. He got up, dazed and confused, only to have the insane waterfowl take a second run at him, knocking him down again. I know this is all true, because it was captured by the security cameras, much to his dismay, a dismay that stemmed more from the cigarette than the goose from what I understand (we weren't actually allowed to see the camera footage, but having it described to us was more than enough to send us into fits of hysterical laughter).

Then, about two weeks later, I read in the paper about a guy who was charged with "wildlife harassment" because he was caught jumping out of a moving boat onto the back of a moose. And by caught, I mean he was stupid enough to post the video on YouTube (there's a surprise—a guy trying to play rodeo with a full-sized moose being stupid?), and someone reported it. The moose looked genuinely terrified, not unlike my co-worker. But here's the thing—a guy who scares a moose faces charges, but a goose who attacks a helpless man gets off scot-free? I'm seeing a bit of a double standard here. The Canada goose is our national bird, and you can't legally kill one, but still—it should have at least been fined.

CHAPTER 5: TIME'S A-TICKING

Anyone who knows me knows about my obsession with clocks. I have a lot of them, 57 at the latest count (most of them don't work—they're just for decoration and most of them are very small), and Ken loves to tease me about it:

Ken: So tomorrow Daylight Savings Time starts, so I went around the house and changed all the clocks...
Me: What do you mean, ALL the clocks?!
Ken: I set all the clocks to the right time. It took me ages to fix the ones in the downstairs bathroom. There's like fifteen of them.
Me: YOU CHANGED ALL THE TIMES ON MY VINTAGE ALARM CLOCK COLLECTION?
Ken: Hahaha. Just kidding.
Me: If only that was even remotely funny, KEN.

Because the whole point of the collection is that each clock presents the time when it finally stopped for good, like a metaphor for death—it's PERFORMANCE ART, KEN. But like most things in my life, my clocks are also strange/possibly haunted. One Friday, as I was getting ready for the day, I looked up at the clocks in my bathroom. They both said 11:34, and it completely freaked me out. Why? I hear you asking. Shouldn't the clocks both be telling the same time? And the answer would normally be yes, but in this case, one clock works and the other DOES NOT. And isn't it an amazingly strange coincidence, or a harbinger of doom perhaps, that I happened to look at both of them when they were showing the same time? Or maybe it was a good omen, I don't know. At any rate, nothing particularly good or bad happened the rest of the day, and also don't judge me for not getting ready for the day until almost noon, because I'm ON MY HOLIDAYS. (Speaking of holidays, Ken and I recently went on a Mediterranean cruise and the one souvenir I brought back was a vintage alarm clock from an antique market in Cannes. I had to put it in my carry-on because Ken was convinced that if airport security saw it in my checked bag, they would think it was a bomb and destroy my suitcase. I also got a tattoo, but that's another story).

Anyway, then I started looking around the house at all the clocks. It's a very large old Victorian house, built in 1906, complete with a front staircase AND a back staircase, which is apparently fascinating to young children who will spend hours doing a circuit involving going up the front stairs, running through the upstairs of the house, going down the back stairs, and running through the main floor of the house. Then repeat. I know this because over the last few days, we've hosted several children who all took tremendous delight in this activity which, I have to admit, is pretty fun and I do it myself on occasion. In fact, I did it on Saturday as I was clock counting.

You may be surprised, and somewhat alarmed (best pun ever) to learn that I have 57 clocks in random places around my house (and I'm not even counting phone, computer, microwave or TV clocks). 18 of them work, and 39 do not. 1 of them is actually just in a drawer. And out of the 39 that don't work, I found three more that had stopped around 11:34-ish, and another two that had stopped at 6:57, which looks frighteningly like 11:34-ish from a distance. I should probably mention at this point that the great majority of my collection consists of vintage alarm clocks and most of them are wind-up, and do I have time to wind up 39 clocks? No, I don't. Plus all that ticking would drive me crazy. But why are some of my clocks fixated around the 11:34-ish mark? Is that when the ghost in my house died? I may never know, but anytime something either wonderful or terrible happens, I'll be sure to look at one of the working clocks to see what time it is.

Me: What time was it when you ate all the cake? I know it was you, so stop trying to blame "the fairies".
The Dog: Fine, fine. You left at 11:30. It was a few minutes after that.
Me: Are you feeling sick yet?
The Dog: A little. I'll probably throw up tomorrow morning, say around 11:34.
Me (whispers): Harbinger of doom…

WHAT ANY NORMAL PERSON WOULD DO

The quest for clocks is not, however, without its dangers:

1) Last Mother's Day

I woke up and after a few minutes, I looked at my phone. There was a new notification from Facebook Marketplace exhorting me to check out the latest thing they had decided was "Just For Me". And obviously, it was a clock. But not just ANY clock—a mid-1800s gingerbread clock, and it was only $10! So I contacted the seller and made arrangements to pick it up—he gave me the address and described his house as 'white with a blue roof'. I was about to leap out of bed, but then Ken came in with a card, inside of which was an assortment of LCBO gift cards, and if you don't live in Ontario, LCBO stands for Liquor Control Board of Ontario, and that's what they do. They control the sale of liquor here, and you can only buy it from their stores or other 'official' outlets instead of at grocery stores and corner stores and off people on the street like you can almost everywhere else in the world. But now I was flush with the potential of buying a lot of wine, so I demanded that Ken take me clock-shopping:

Ken: But you already have 54 clocks.
Me: Most of them don't EVEN WORK, KEN.
Ken: But I was going to make a little wooden boat and put this plastic lion on it.
Me: That's very cute. But the clock is just up the road, and coming with me can make up for you not bringing me breakfast in bed.
Ken: Sigh. Fine.

Me: Great! Also, I bought a jigsaw puzzle from someone in Brantford, so if we leave now, we can feed two birds with one…bag of birdseed or whatever.
Ken: You mean, kill two birds with--
Me: NO.

So off we went. I had put the address into my GPS, and it directed us to a house. A white house with a blue roof. But the number on the house was different than the address the guy had given me, so I messaged him:

Me: We're here but the number doesn't match. Can you resend the house number?
Guy: It's the white house with the blue roof.
Me: We're here!

I rang the bell, and I saw a woman through the window scurrying around inside, but she didn't come to the door. I rang the bell again, and she yelled, "That door is locked!" and I was like, "Okay, I'm just here for the clock!" Then she poked her head out the side door and yelled, "I don't have a clock!" and slammed the door.

By this point, I was a little frustrated and also feeling gangster-y, about to yell, "Give me the clock and no one gets hurt!" but then Ken realized that the guy lived to the north of the highway and we were south and I was like, "Is that up or down from here?", but long story short, we found the guy's house, and wouldn't you know it—it was also WHITE WITH A BLUE ROOF.

Then we went to Brantford and picked up the jigsaw puzzle and made it back home within the hour. And within that very hour, our dog decided that the remote controls for our satellite dish and our streaming stick were exactly the thing for a mid-morning snack. We walked into the house, clock and puzzle in hand, and were greeted by shards of plastic strewn all over the family room. And out of the four AAA batteries involved in this scenario, WE COULD ONLY FIND 3.

So that's how I spent my Mother's Day—terrified that my dog was going to die. As for him, he was quite nonchalant about the whole ordeal:

Me: What's wrong with you?! Those aren't food!
The Dog: Says you. They were quite tasty.
Me: You could get really sick!
The Dog: Meh, I feel fine now. I can't guarantee how this will play out around 11:34 though.

At any rate, it was a crazy time. We never did find the battery, either in the house or in his poo, but he seemed perfectly fine, and based on the sheer quantity of the poo that he managed to squeeze out over the next seven days, it didn't appear that he had a blockage. But now, whenever I want to watch Netflix, I have to push his nose.

2) PSST, Wanna Buy A Clock?

Now that I'm retired, I work part-time in an antique market. There are a lot of vendors, and one of the rules is that if they bring anything to their booths, they have to "sell it through the till", which is to say, they can't offer staff a good deal. Officially. Because I'd been working there for a couple of months when this happened:

I was at the side door just about to go in to work when a guy pulled up and started to unload a van. I didn't know who the dude was, and I didn't really care because my attention was IMMEDIATELY focused on the gorgeous clock on the top of the bin he had put on the ground:

Me: I like your clock.
Dude: It's for sale.
Me: How much?
Dude: Forty bucks.
Me: Great! Can I buy it?
Dude: If you want it, you need to take it NOW and put it in your car. GO. NOW. Before anyone sees you! RUN!!
Me: How do I pay you for it?
Dude (looking around wildly, for what I wasn't sure): You can e-transfer me later—just go!!

And even though I had no idea who he was, or how I could e-transfer a paranoid stranger, I picked the very heavy, 2-foot-high clock up in my arms and hightailed it across the parking lot like a middle-aged Nancy Drew. You would have thought I was buying cocaine rather than a 75-year-old timepiece, although to me, a 75-year-old timepiece is as good, if not better, than cocaine. I safely stowed the clock in the back of my car, covering it with a blanket just in case the clock detectives came by. I didn't see the dude for the rest of the day and was wondering what to do about paying for my illicit purchase, when he suddenly appeared. He wrote something quickly on a piece of newspaper and handed it to me surreptitiously.

Me: Awesome. It was forty dollars, right?

Dude (looks around to see if anyone is listening): SHHH. Don't send the transfer until you get home, in case anyone sees you.

Me: Uh…okay.

Dude: By the way, the clock doesn't work.

Me: Do clocks ever really work? Time is a human construct…

Dude: We can't be seen talking!

But then I looked at the piece of paper and I couldn't read his writing. I wasn't sure what to do, but right before the end of the day, he appeared again:

Me: I'm having trouble reading your handwriting. So is your last name--

Dude: SHHHH!! Come this way with me. Is anyone watching?

Me: No…?

Dude: Pretend you're walking with me to the back to open the door.

Me: AM I opening the door for you?

Dude: That's what we'll tell people if they see us.

So I went with him to the back and he whisper-spelled the email address to me, then disappeared out the door. I never saw him again.

That night, while Ken watched TV, I lay in bed next to him staring at my new clock, which I'd placed on a table in our bedroom alcove, along with some of my other favourite things: a small Persian mat, a Paris painting, a lamp with a stained-glass shade, and some old poetry books.

Me: Sigh. I love you.

Ken: I love you too.

Me (confused because I wasn't actually talking to Ken): Yes, right. Do you know what else I love?

Ken: What?

Me: That f*cking clock. But I love you, Kate, and the dog more. Obviously.

Ken (laughs): Obviously.

WHAT ANY NORMAL PERSON WOULD DO

CHAPTER 6: BATHROOM TALES

I have to admit that I have a strange obsession with bathrooms. For some reason, I tend to write about them (the bathrooms themselves, not the bodily functions that OCCUR in them, thankfully) a LOT. I think it stems from the fact that in my former career as a teacher, I could only use the bathroom at certain times during the day. And while there were many bathrooms for the students, there was only one staff bathroom. That could be very awkward since I taught 3 floors away from the staff bathroom, and most often resorted to using the girls' bathroom down the hall from my classroom, in order to be more efficient. As a side note, are there any other professions where you can't go to the bathroom when you want to? When a BELL tells you when it's okay to pee?

But let's face facts; most of us had a 'system', a type of rotating coverage where we kept an eye on each other's classes in the case of an emergency, and since our classes were made up of teenagers, it was a pretty safe bet that you could nip out for a quickie without anything bad happening, like someone putting glue in someone else's hair, or poking each other until someone cried, or whatever. I haven't taught elementary school in a while, but I know those kids get into trouble at the drop of a hat (or a number 2). Kindergarten teachers must have to hold it ALL DAY—what a life. As a second side note, when I used the staff bathroom, it was almost inevitable that another staff member (usually female—well, always female, really) would want to strike up a conversation when I was trying to do something that required both privacy and a certain amount of concentration. I NEVER had that problem in the girls' bathroom. On a third side note, I never made my students ask to go to the bathroom. They were allowed to just leave. I have no interest in being in charge of anyone else's bowels, and the whole notion of someone asking me "Can I go to the bathroom?" tweaks the absurdist part of my brain. Is there really more than one response to that question? Why would I EVER say No? Some people might ask, "But how do you know they're really going to the bathroom?" What the hell else would they be doing? Starting an insurrection? Holding cockfighting tournaments in the basement? Basically, I trusted my students to do what they said they were going to do, until I actually found them NOT doing it. Or they came back to my room covered in feathers.

One of the joys of using a student bathroom is that you never knew what kind of surprise was awaiting you. There was usually a lot of graffiti, although the custodians did their best to remove it regularly. Girl graffiti is a bit boring, mostly stuff like "Johnny is so hot", or "School sucks". Last year, there was a whole thread about the power of the Lord, and living your life like Jesus. It's amazing the kind of pious sentiments that bodily functions can provoke. But I worked in a school with a large International Baccalaureate program, so sometimes the graffiti was fairly esoteric. One day, for example, I sat down in a stall, and read the following:

Things I Hate
1. Vandelism
2. Irony
3. Lists
4. Originality
5. Poor spelling

It made me laugh, and I wondered what was going on in this girl's life at that moment, what prompted her to take black sharpie to the back of a bathroom stall door. But kids do weird things in bathrooms. When I was 16, we got up to all kinds of things, mostly smoking. You'd skip out of class, meet up with a friend and have a smoke. Teachers regularly came in to check the bathrooms back then—not to actually USE them, but just to see what we were up to—and sometimes they caught you smoking and you got sent to the office, and sometimes they just shook their heads sympathetically at you and left. Nowadays, girls never seem to smoke in the bathroom. Which is why one day, I was so confused and befuddled. I came out of a stall, was washing my hands with the outrageously cold water that the students are gifted with, and I saw a girl at the hand dryer, having an animated conversation with another girl about a boy she liked, and she was DRYING A CIGARETTE LIGHTER. Very casually, like there was nothing strange about this at all. Based on my own life experiences, however, I immediately jumped to "She skipped class to go have a smoke, dropped her lighter in a snowbank, and was now trying to dry it off in order to resume her smoking. And tonight is PARENTS' NIGHT!" So, being the responsible adult that I am, I, equally casually, but just a little bit ominously, went over and asked, "Hi there. Can you tell me why you're drying a cigarette lighter?"

She gave me a big smile and replied, "Oh, we're doing an experiment in Chemistry and it fell into the beaker." So now I felt like a complete dick, being all suspicious of this poor young scientist type—it just goes to show you that teenagers are, for the most part, pretty decent human beings if you don't pre-judge them. I mean, look at me—I turned out all right…

Then, that Friday, I had my second weird bathroom experience in the same week. I went in and there was no one around, but taped to the front of the first stall was a handwritten note that said, "Do Not Flush. Ring in toilet." Now in my experience, toilet rings are best removed by a good scrub and a flush, so naturally I was intrigued. I looked, and sure enough, there was an actual ring in the toilet—a gold ring. It looked slightly like the Ring of Power from Lord of the Rings, and I simultaneously felt like whispering "My Precious" and then seeking out the girl with the lighter to see if we could heat it up and make some runes appear on it. The toilet water looked clean enough though, and I hated the thought that this stall would become permanently unusable, while everyone avoided flushing the ring, so I did what any normal person (as it turns out, not really) would do—I pushed up my sleeve, stuck my hand in the toilet, and pulled the ring out. Then I washed it, and my hands, a couple of times just to be sure. It turned out to be a piece of costume jewelry, but it might have had some sentimental value, so I rewrote the note, directing people who were interested in it to my classroom, wrapped it in some toilet paper, and took it to my room.

"Look what I found!" I exclaimed to some of my grade 12 students.

"Oh my god," they replied. "Did you pull that out of the toilet?!" Apparently, it had been in there long enough that a lot of the girls had seen it.

"The water was clean," I said. "Besides, I've changed dirty diapers and cleaned up baby puke. My hands have been in worse places."

This, for some reason, did not comfort them, but prompted some of the girls to insist that they were never having children. So I feel like, on the one hand, I did a good deed by saving someone's precious ring, but on the other hand, I might be responsible for declining enrollment.

Then I changed jobs, and as part of that new position, twice a year we had to work off-site, so we needed an extra outdoor bathroom trailer because many of the temporary staff were women and as we all know, women go to the bathroom constantly, especially if they don't think they'll be able to go to the bathroom for a while, even if they don't really need to. So the line-up to the women's bathroom was always extremely long. In the spring, the problem was that the bathroom trailer was never level, but on an angle severe enough that I was afraid to use it for fear of it toppling over. This wouldn't pose a problem except that the windows and doors are always on the side that would hit the ground, thereby trapping me inside and causing me to drown in sewage.

This is weird, yes? But not so weird that I didn't have a pact with a colleague who felt exactly the same way in that we notified each other when we were going out there with the promise: "If I'm not back in 5 minutes, check that the porta-potty hasn't fallen over." But when we arrived at the site for the second session in the summer, she came to me very excited:

Colleague: The portable toilet trailer is here!
Me: Ergh. How bad is the angle?
Colleague: Pretty bad, but it's set up perpendicular to the building this time so instead of toppling over, it would just roll down into the parking lot, hitting a bunch of cars!
Me: THAT is excellent news.
Colleague: I KNOW!!

And I was so happy that there were now better positioned outdoor bathrooms because at the previous session in the spring at the same large convention centre, I'd had to deal with a lot of bathroom shenanigans while avoiding the outdoor toilets. Back at the office, I could time my visits so that there was little chance of anyone else hearing me pee (you can think this is weird if you want, but there are a

LOT of people who find that uncomfortable), but off-site, I had the "pleasure" of using the facilities with a lot of unusual strangers and dealt with a lot of strange bathroom behaviour:

First, there was the woman who kept speaking to the tap. Okay, in fairness, she talked to a lot of things, but the tap must have been the best conversationalist of the bunch, because they had some pretty intensive debates. I understood that she had mental health issues, but it was still disconcerting to be in a stall, overhear two people arguing in angry whispers, come out, and realize there's only one other person in the room. I was fully expecting to find the word REDRUM scrawled on the mirror in lipstick.

One day, I went into the bathroom and a woman hid behind the corner near the hand dryer when she saw me. It freaked me out a little, but then I realized that she was talking on a cell phone. I figured it must be a really private conversation, so I did what I had to (as quietly as I could, of course) then left. About an hour later, one of my colleagues came out of the bathroom looking really worried. When I asked why, she said, "When I went in, some woman ran and hid behind the corner and she stayed there the entire time. It was weird." When I told her the same thing had happened to me but over an hour earlier, we decided to get the security guard to check it out. It turns out that she was one of the facility workers and was trying to avoid doing her job. Which was serving coffee. Yes, I would love a cup of coffee passed to me by someone who has been hanging out in the BATHROOM for two hours.

Next, after almost a week on-site, there was the woman who

asked someone how the tap worked. It was one of those taps where you have to put your hands under it to activate the water. This worried me—how did she go that many days without USING the tap? Icky!

The next day I was in a stall, and suddenly there was a camera flash from the stall next door. What the heck? I looked down and could see the shadow of a cellphone in someone's hands. My first and only thought was that she must be breaching security and taking pictures of confidential material. I lingered at the hand dryer and watched her stall surreptitiously. I could see her moving around and then raising one arm above her head like she was stretching. When she came out though, she wasn't carrying any papers or documents. Strange. When I told my co-workers that I had seen a flash, then saw the shadow look like she was texting the image to someone and that I was worried she was stealing information, they started laughing hysterically.

"She was taking pictures of her ladyparts and sending them to someone!" a colleague exclaimed. "You're so naïve!" (Actually, she said "hoo-hoo" instead of ladyparts, but some of you might not be familiar with that word, hence my substitution of "ladyparts" for clarity). I guess I AM naïve—how sexy is it to take a picture of yourself when you're on the toilet? Is it some kind of *Shades of Grey* thing? Double-icky! There are a lot of people who absolutely refuse to use public bathrooms and now I understand why.

But at least none of these bathrooms were haunted because I've had my fair share of encounters with bathroom ghosts. Once, a group of us from work went to The Keg on Jarvis St. in Toronto to celebrate a colleague's retirement. I love The Keg (a steakhouse chain for anyone who has never been there) for many reasons, but it's mostly because I believe that steak wrapped in bacon is nature's perfect food, and The Keg always cooks it to perfection. Ken and I go to the local Keg on occasion, and of course, Ken always orders salmon. To me, this is like going to Red Lobster and ordering a hamburger. He had a terrible incident a few years ago, when restaurants had somehow all bizarrely decided that salmon should be cooked slightly rare. Because who doesn't like to eat undercooked fish? What's next? Medium rare chicken with a side of salmonella? Anyway, he got quite ill, so now he always asks for his salmon completely cooked, which seems weird that you actually have to specify that.

But I digress. Most Kegs are in fairly modern buildings with new fixtures and stone fireplaces—kind of ski chalet chic. But this particular restaurant on Jarvis St. is known as The Keg Mansion—it's an enormous and beautiful castle-like structure built by members of the McMaster family and then owned by the Massey family (of Massey Hall fame). The best part about the whole business is that the Keg Mansion is also known as "The Haunted Mansion", because apparently there have been numerous sightings of ghosts, spirits, and other presences over the years.

Call me crazy, but I LOVE ghostly type things, so I couldn't wait to go there. As we were finishing our dinner, two of the women I was sitting with started talking about the second-floor bathroom being haunted by a presence of some kind. We may or may not have been drinking a little, so we decided to make a visit to the ladies room to check it out. Up we went, giggling like schoolgirls and found the haunted bathroom. We were expecting something amazing, like the bathroom in *Harry Potter* where the ghost of that crazy-ass Myrtle chick comes out of the tap, but we were sadly disappointed. It wasn't even a very NICE bathroom—kind of industrial beige and a bit grubby. We hung around for a bit, but nothing happened so we went back downstairs to our table. "Well," I said, "that was nothing like the ghost in the bathroom of the house where I used to live." Heads all turned. "What ghost?!" they wanted to know. So I told them the story I'm about to tell you now. And it's all true...

When Ken and I were first married, we lived in one side of a 100-year-old "twin home", which is like a semi-detached house. The old basement didn't LOOK creepy but it felt that way, like someone was watching you, and I avoided going down there like the plague. After a couple of months, we moved into the OTHER side of the house. Same layout, same type and age of basement, only I had no problem going down there at all. No bad vibes whatsoever. A few years later, we bought a house in Washington (Ontario, not DC). It was a huge old Georgian-style place, built in 1863, and pretty run down, having been empty for almost two years after the 80-year-old owner had passed away. We began renovating right away, starting with the upstairs bathroom, which had been built into a back bedroom which became Kate's room. The walls were clad in pressure-treated boards. It had a wall sink, a clawfoot tub, and a swag lamp for lighting. Totally creepy, dark, and dingy.

After redoing the walls with board and batten, painting the whole thing white and updating the fixtures (including a new medicine cabinet), it was much more livable. For me AND for the obnoxious poltergeist who occupied it. Yes, I said "poltergeist", and it was one with a very juvenile sense of humour. It wasn't long before things started flying out of the new medicine cabinet. And I don't mean "falling out", I mean a kind of forceful lobbing. If I had a dollar for every time I got hit with a hairbrush, or my toothbrush flew into the toilet, I'd be a rich woman. There was a built-in cupboard in the corner with upper and lower doors—sometimes if you bent down to get something out of the lower cabinet, when you went to stand up the upper doors would be suddenly open and you'd crack your head on them. Every so often, I'd get really pissed off and yell, "Cut it out, stupid ghost!!" and for a week or two, there would be no incidents. Of course, Ken was totally skeptical, having his own POLTERGEIST-FREE bathroom on the main floor. "Maybe the gravity is just weird in there," he'd say. "Or maybe the walls are on an angle or something." But it wasn't always confined to the bathroom—every once in a while, the guest bedroom next door would smell like cigarette smoke, even though no one in the house smoked.

Now, you might think this was all in my imagination but here's why I know it wasn't. A few years later, we moved down the road to the town where we still live. One summer Saturday morning, we were having a garage sale, and a very elderly man drove up. He struck up a conversation with us, said that he'd lived in our area all his life and that he knew the woman who used to own our new old (1906) house quite well. I told him we used to live in Washington in the "big, red house on the corner."

"I know the place," he said. "My uncle Len lived there for most of his life, before the people you bought from. He was over eighty when he died. He got really 'funny' towards the last part of his life—a real practical joker. His favourite trick was to put on a devil's mask, then sneak up to the church when the ladies' choir was practicing. He'd peek in the windows and just about scare them to death, then run away laughing! Of course, it was the cancer that got him in the end—he was a chain smoker, you know." And for a long time, I was pretty salty about all the toothbrushes, but then I used the whole situation as inspiration for part of my third novel so I figure Uncle Len and I are even.

Another time, I THOUGHT a bathroom was haunted but it really wasn't. I was having dinner with my cousin, and we were at a restaurant I'd never been to before and when we'd finished eating, I excused myself to go to the ladies room. I walked into the stall (there were only two, so I chose the one that seemed the most ghost-free), but the toilet looked very strange. I stared at it for a second, then the lid started to go up. ALL BY ITSELF. I had a moment of panic where I thought I had made a fatal, haunted mistake, but then I realized that the toilet had these warm, glowing blue and red lights. It was a ROBOT TOILET.

I hesitated for a second, but I really had to go, so I sat down. There was what seemed to be a control bar on the wall next to the toilet, and I didn't have my reading glasses on, but in a completely devil-may-care moment, I decided to push one of the buttons. Suddenly, I was being sprayed by jets of warm water. It was delightful.

The problem, however, was that it was completely body temperature and after a minute or two, I couldn't tell anymore whether the "water" was coming from me or the toilet and it seemed like I had been sitting there for a lot longer than necessary. I had no idea how to stop it, so I tried standing up in the hope that the spray was also motion-activated like the lid or something, but it wasn't, and the higher I got, the higher the jets got, and I didn't want to get soaked so I sat back down.

Not knowing what else to do, I started pushing the other buttons on the wall-mounted bar. Apparently, the first one controlled the water pressure and the water was now more like a geyser than a gentle fountain. The next one controlled the position of the spray, and I had now gone from front to back—it was incredibly aggressive and somewhat "invasive" and I was starting to worry that I would never get out of the stall in one piece. Another one made the toilet seat heat up. The last button played classical music, because why the f*ck not? So there I was, on a hot toilet seat, my nether regions being blasted by jets of tepid water to the strains of Tchaikovsky when I finally found the "off" button. After I'd dried off, I came out of the bathroom laughing hysterically, so much so that I could barely explain to my cousin what had happened.

Me: OH MY GOD. That was the best toilet I've ever sat on!
Cousin: Okay.
Me: I totally need one for my house!
Cousin: Okay then.

And then of course, there was the time I realized that the bathroom at my own office was haunted. On a Thursday afternoon, not long after lunch, I walked down the hall to the bathroom. Things were pretty quiet, it being a snow day and everything, so not a lot of people were around. I took the time to stop and congratulate the receptionist, a lovely younger woman, on her recent engagement. We chatted for a bit, then I continued on my way. I opened the outer door to the facilities, and then pushed at the inner door, at which point I realized that the motion-sensitive lights were off. As they began to come on, I heard the most terrifying noise—it sounded like someone in the first stall was freaking out and slamming the toilet paper dispenser. I could see a shadow flickering, and thought for a second that it was the building's custodian replacing the roll or something, but then I realized that there was NO ONE IN THE STALL. Without even thinking, I tore out of there like a bat out of hell and ran around behind the reception desk, shaking.

"What happened?!" asked the receptionist.

"There's something in the bathroom!" I said, hyperventilating.

"What are you talking about? What's in the bathroom?! I thought I heard banging—what was it?!" she demanded.

"I don't know, but there's definitely something in there!"

I described to her what happened, and after a minute, she agreed to go back in with me and check it out. This was NOT a decision that either of us took lightly, and we tiptoed to the door, and very cautiously re-opened it. "Where was the noise coming from?" she asked.

"The first stall," I answered. "Oh my god, not the first stall!" she exclaimed. "That stall is haunted! The receptionist who used to work here told me that!"

At which point, we both ran out of the bathroom back to the reception desk. "I can't go back in there," I said. "What am I going to do? I really need to go."

"Use the one downstairs," she said. "Here's the code."

So I went downstairs, but it was almost as bad, maybe because I was still shaken up. The door creaked like someone crying, which terrified me, and there was a dark room at the back with a couch in it that I had to check first to make sure no one was hiding in it.

The rest of the afternoon was stressful. My work partner had left to visit her parents, and I needed to use the bathroom one more time before I got on the train, but there was no one to come with me. I wandered past reception again, hoping that I could catch someone going in the 'bathroom of death' and wander in behind her. I was in luck—another co-worker was chatting with the receptionist.

"You wouldn't happen to be on your way to the ladies' room?" I asked.

"I was…why?" she asked suspiciously. "What's going on?"

I was looking hedgy, and the receptionist was giggling. "Oh, nothing. I just had something weird happen earlier, and it spooked me out a little."

I explained to her what happened, and she said, "Oh, I know what that was!"

We went into the bathroom, and without fear or hesitation, she opened the door to the first stall. "See the automated sanitary disposal? It's broken. When the overhead lights come on, it triggers the sensor in the lid, and it flaps up and down like crazy. Makes a terrible noise." She demonstrated, and sure enough, that was what I heard. I sagged in relief, then we both looked at each other and started to laugh hysterically. We went back out to the reception area and told the receptionist what had happened.

"Oh, no," she said. "That's not what the other woman used to say. She said that the door to the stall would swing open and shut all by itself."

My co-worker and I looked at each other nervously. "Must just be the wind," I said, and we all agreed to agree.

But that wasn't the only time I struggled with a bathroom at work. We had the staff bathroom but we also had a big conference room that used to be the CEO's office. There was a bathroom in there designed exclusively for the CEO and it came fully equipped—it even had a shower. But then we got a new CEO who felt that having his own private bathroom was too ostentatious, so he took a smaller office and gave the rest of us the use of the conference room and accompanying bathroom. I was in there for a meeting one day and it went on for a while. I'd been drinking a LOT of green tea that morning, so when we got to the last item on the agenda, I said, "Will this be a long one? I have to use the Ladies, so if the answer's 'Yes', I'll pop out really quickly."

The director said, "Oh, just use the one in here." I was hesitant but they all made jokes about how no one would listen to me. Still, for good measure, I turned the faucet on high just to drown out any obvious noise. When I was finished, I stood up, turned around, and was at a complete loss. There was no discernable way to flush the toilet. No lever, no handle, no button, nothing. I didn't know what to do. I couldn't stay in there forever—I mean, I was in the middle of a f*cking meeting. People were LITERALLY waiting for me to come out. So finally, I opened the door and stood there.

Director: What's wrong?
Me: I—I don't know how to flush the toilet…
Everyone: What?!
Me: There's no mechanism that I can see whatsoever. I don't know how to flush it.

One of the managers jumped up and came into the bathroom with me. She looked around and pressed a switch. The lights went off. She turned the lights back on, then we both stood there looking at the toilet.

Manager: She's right. There's no handle.
Director (coming over): No, there has to be.

Then we all stood there staring at the mysterious porcelain repository. Finally, the director crouched down and looked around. "I think I see something!" she said. She reached behind the toilet and pushed a button, at which point the damned thing flushed, and everyone dissolved into hysterical laughter.

Director: And now we all know how to flush this toilet.
Me: Yup.

But aside from the grandiose conference room bathroom, I know you're dying to find out which bathroom stall at work was my favourite...

Ah, now THAT is an excellent question. At work, there were five stalls in the ladies bathroom. Stall 5 was my favourite, because it was against the far wall with no other stall to the left, so if stall 4 was empty, I ALWAYS used Stall 5. But then I noticed that the toilet paper in Stall 5 ran out not long after lunch while the other stalls still had their full complement, which led me to the inevitable conclusion that Stall 5 was also the favourite bathroom stall of a whole lot of other people. And I didn't want to use the same bathroom stall as everyone else because I liked to imagine that when I sat down, I was sitting on a pristine seat, and that's impossible to do when you know that it's being overused compared to the other stalls. Hence my decision to change my favourite stall to Stall 4.

However, if Stall 4 was occupied, then I immediately went to Stall 2 if the ones on either side were both empty. I NEVER used Stall 1 because, as we have established, a ghost lived in it. I WOULD use Stall 3 in an absolute emergency.

Bathroom Stall Overall Ranking:

5: 3 (but only in the morning before the lunchtime rush)

2: 2

4: 1

3: 4

1: Boo.

Then, of course, in the spring of 2020, we were all sent home for a couple of weeks, which turned into a couple of years, and I no longer had to worry about the bathrooms at work. In honour of working from home, I present to you the bathrooms in my house in order of least to most favourite:

4) Upstairs back of the house

This bathroom is nice, but it's narrow and far away from my office. Also, like Stall 1 at work, a ghost lives in it. I know this because the lights flicker, and strange things happen in the adjacent bedroom, like paintings falling off the walls. Also, there's a small sliding door in the bathroom wall—there was a vent pipe inside that led into the closet in the haunted bedroom directly behind the bathroom. Last year, we were cleaning out the bedroom closet and realized the pipe just went directly from the bathroom into the closet floor and stopped there, so we pulled it out and discovered the most bizarre collection of things under the floor of the closet that someone in the past had thrown down the pipe in the bathroom, obviously not realizing that it wasn't a MAGICAL pipe. There was a pair of boy's underwear, a love letter written to the son of the previous occupant ("Hi Jordan, If you lik me, rite back" with a heart drawn in crayon. I guess he didn't "lik" her since he threw the letter into the magic pipe) and a couple of condom wrappers, so maybe he changed his mind at some point? The weirdest thing was about 9 pairs of old panty hose, and I can't even begin to explain THAT, having not owned a pair of panty hose for over twenty years, long before we bought this house. Maybe the ghost was a fancy woman.

3) Main floor bathroom slash laundry room

This bathroom is very utilitarian, housing the laundry facilities as well. However, the knee-to cabinet ratio is a little tight for me. This is "Ken's bathroom". It has a nice shower, but I'm a bath girl. The last time I used that shower was the day I ran a gas-powered pressure sprayer over my foot. Ken carried me screaming into the shower to get the dirt out of my flayed toes because it was the closest bathroom to the incident. So it's very handy in a medical emergency.

2) Main floor back powder room

This is the bathroom where I keep part of my infamous vintage clock collection. You'll remember that I have a lot of old clocks that don't work scattered around the house, but this bathroom is where space and time converge. Also, I made a toilet paper holder out of an old piano stool base and a curtain rod, and at the time, people thought it was very ostentatious, but given the fact that not long after I made it, toilet paper became as rare as rhodium, I think it was a fitting tribute.

I like this bathroom well enough, and it's close to the back family room where we watch movies. You can dash to the toilet and still hear the dialogue if you keep the door slightly open. Much better acoustics than a movie theatre bathroom and much cleaner.

1) Master Ensuite

This is MY bathroom, and it's the best one in the house as far as I'm concerned. It's like Stall 5 at work, if Stall 5 was never used by anyone but me. It's technically an ensuite for the master bedroom but it belongs to ME. It also has a balcony (not very high off the ground) that you can sit out on in the summer, which is random for a bathroom, but this whole house has been reconfigured several times over the last 114 years, and apparently the bathroom used to be a kitchen when the upstairs of the house was 2 apartments. Ken and I renovated it a couple of years ago. Originally, the walls were covered with giant damask roses, which I loved but which Ken CONSTANTLY complained about, so I finally gave in when we found all these doors for free at the side of the road and he proposed that we create a wall of doors. My favourite thing is the stained-glass window panel we installed. Also, it's the place where I create characters such as Captain John Crapper and Princess Toilette, using my toilet and other accessories.

Also, if you're wondering why on earth we have FOUR bathrooms for two people, let me just say that our house is in a very small town far from the city, and when we bought it almost 18 years ago (when Kate was still at home), the price was incredibly low compared to what we could have gotten for the same money in a larger city. Now that we're both retired, we're thinking of turning it into a bed and breakfast, or a writing/photography retreat. As long as nobody moves my stuff or changes my clocks, it'll be great.

Of course, the main reason my bathroom is always going to be my favourite is because I only have a bathtub, and no shower, which makes me very happy because I hate showers. Here are some reasons why showers are the worst thing ever:

1) Showers are creatures of evil.

They were invented by someone who thought, "Mwah haha! How can I make people miserable and uncomfortable while they are trying to soap up and rinse parts of their body they can't see?! I know—how about making them stand under stinging, randomly placed pricks of water? And to make it even better, the temperature of the water will fluctuate between ice-cold and scalding hot whenever someone else flushes the toilet. This is perfect!! Mwah haha!" Screw you, shower-inventor and your malevolent plans. Also, the other reason you can tell that showers are evil is that no one EVER baptized an adult by making them stand under a bucket of water. No, it's total immersion for the healthy soul, people. Yes, I know babies have water sprinkled on their heads, and this is why babies HATE showers. Well, sensible babies, anyway.

2) Showers are terrible for the visually-impaired.

I hate showers now, after my laser eye surgery, because they're devil-spawn, but originally, I hated showers because I was almost legally blind. I couldn't wear contact lenses while I was showering because the force of the water running down my face would knock them out and send them down the drain. If I DIDN'T wear contact lenses, I couldn't see ANYTHING, including what I was using to wash my hair. In fact, once at a hotel, I reached out and instead of the tiny conditioner bottle, I grabbed the body lotion (because when you're blind as a bat, the words 'conditioner' and 'body lotion' are pretty much identical) and slathered it all over my hair, and let me tell you, that sh*t was hard to get out. And I couldn't wear glasses, because the other stupid thing that a shower does is…

3) Showers create steam.

So on top of having to suffer through the torment of hot water, cold air, and then groping for your towel while water is dripping down your face and into your ears, you have to claw through clouds of fog to find a place to sit down and dry your feet. And the only place is the toilet. So there you are, sitting on a plastic toilet seat, trying to dry yourself off, shivering from the cold, and wondering what you did to deserve this misery. Bathtubs, of course, have a ledge which is perfectly designed to perch on while you towel off, still all warm and toasty inside from being immersed in glorious hot water.

4) Showers are noisy.

How am I supposed to relax at the end of the day with the thunderous sound of water in my ears? Loud noises stress me out terribly, but at least with the bath, I can run it with the door shut, then get in and enjoy the quiet solitude. I don't even let the water run out until I'm completely finished, just to preserve the sense of calm. Unlike a shower, where you go from the cacophony of the water to the chaos of the shower fan. It's like some kind of medieval witch torture scenario—you're naked, cold, half-drowned, and the mob/ceiling vent fan is screaming at you but you can't see them through all the fog. Also, when you're in the shower, with all the noise and the shower curtain obscuring your vision, you have NO IDEA if a serial killer is in your bathroom. I learned this from "Psycho" and I've never forgotten it.

5) Showers take away my autonomy.

I like to CHOOSE what parts of me get wet. (And if, right now, you're all like, "Ooh—that's what SHE said," then you're obviously a shower person.)

As far as I'm concerned, there's nothing better than soaking in a tub full of hot water to make you feel clean and shiny. Of course, there are people who don't understand this. In fact, I was complaining to Ken about it after we got back from our last trip. We stayed in a 'luxury' hotel that did NOT have any bathtubs in their rooms, and how is that luxury in any possible f*cking sense of the word?!:

Me: I hate showers. I'm so happy I'm home, and I can finally have a bath.
Ken: I don't understand how you enjoy sitting in your own dirty water. It's like swimming in a cesspool.
Me: What?! How the hell is it a "cesspool"? What do you think I DO all day? I work in an office. I'm not a f*cking mud wrestler! I

don't even sweat! How insulting.

Ken: I'd rather have a shower.

Me: Philistine.

CHAPTER 7: OCD MUCH?

One thing you may have already guessed about me is that I have OCD. My OCD, which is usually fairly mild, flares up when I'm stressed out. It isn't bad most days—in fact, you might not even notice it, unless you look around my house and realize that all objects of décor are organized in specific patterns, or you've watched me put groceries on the conveyer belt according to size and shape and with one inch of space between all items, or you've seen me in the bathroom washing my hands simply because doing that fills me with a sense of profound relief, or you've noticed my dermatophagia. One of the things that helps calm me down when I'm feeling very anxious is looking at an analogue clock. And when I'm REALLY anxious, I do what any normal person would do—I buy a clock. And as you already know, I have A LOT of clocks so you can imagine how much anxiety I regularly deal with.

As a person with OCD, I have a few quirks, aside from buying a lot of clocks. One of them, which a lot of people don't understand, is that I can't stand to touch library books. The idea of the hundreds, maybe thousands of people who have touched the book before me, in all kinds of unsavoury circumstances (it's amazing how many people like to read on the toilet) make me feel icky, which is a technical, medical term for 'uncomfortable, like I really need to wash my hands'. Once, I was looking at a friend's book, and I really wanted to know what it was about, but I couldn't bring myself to touch the cover so that I could open it to read the synopsis. I resorted to saying, "That book looks interesting. What's it about?" and she replied, "Here, take a look," and tried to hand it to me.

I reacted in an externally reasonable way, which was NOT to yell, "No! Don't let it touch me!" Instead, I said, "Oh, but it would be so much better if you gave me YOUR impression of it." And then she laughed, because she remembered that I have an issue with library books, which I MIGHT have mentioned once (maybe more than once), and she told me what the book was about instead of making me touch it. See, now THAT's a friend. Although, she's also the person who told me about finding bed bugs in a library book last year, and now she always leaves them outside for few hours to make sure any bugs are dead, so in a way, she also contributed to my fear of library books. Oh well, six of one, half a dozen of the other, right?

Ken barely notices my 'quirks', but every once in a while they becomes VERY apparent, like this incident a few years ago:

Me: WHAT THE F*CK?!

Ken: What's wrong?!

Me: The little clock goes on the right! The RIGHT!! Why can't she remember that? It's not difficult! There are only two directions—right and left. The little clock always goes on the right!! At a certain point, you've got to think she's doing it on purpose!

Ken: Sigh.

The "she" in question was our new house cleaner. Now, before you start lumping me in with the Kardashians, like I have so much money that I could afford a maid, let me clarify that she only came in once every two weeks, just to do the basics. With me away for work all week, and only seeing Ken on the weekends, the last thing we wanted to do was spend all day Saturday cleaning the house. Plus, I needed to write, and dusting got in the way of that. Obviously, a dirty house is a problem for me, hence hiring someone to help out. The cleaner was young and relatively inexpensive, but also apparently oblivious to the order of things. The first week that she came, she had left the cupboards in the kitchen in total disarray, causing me to have a small breakdown.

"She moved EVERYTHING!!" I cried to Ken. He kindly suggested I get out the photographs so that I could put everything back. Yes, photographs. I take photographs of the way I've arranged things so that I know how to put them back, just in case. It's especially helpful at Christmas, when I want to place ornaments in the exact same position as the year previous. So I spent a good hour putting things back where they were supposed to be. Eventually, I got used to the fact that every other weekend, I would come home to subtle disarray, but there was also some stress-relief involved as I re-ordered my world and then stood back and admired the renewed symmetry.

I also have a lot of hygiene issues—that goes without saying. The only time I was ever at a strip club was when I went, ironically, to a Chippendales show for a friend's stag-ette party. The guys came out, all sweaty and gyrating, and the women went wild. But then the guys started shoving T-shirts down their sweaty pants and throwing them to women in the crowd. My OCD hygiene issues kicked in full force and I literally had to leave, running and dodging as I went. The ONLY good thing about that night was that the doorman asked me for ID. (I related this story to my tattoo artist/former Chippendales dancer and he responded with "I know. We used to be so much more classy.)

And of course, the hygiene issues extend to other areas, like my obsession with the 'good' tea towel, and don't tell me you've never had one of those because unless you're under 25, you definitely have, and even if you're under 25, if you're anything like me at all, you've had one since you were 13. Normally at home, it hasn't been an issue—Ken and Kate have always, at least until recently, respected the good tea towel, which is to say, the tea towel that hangs on a rack for purely decorative reasons and should NEVER be used. If you are not familiar with the concept of the good tea towel, let me explain. There are the tea towels that you use every day, the ones you dry things with, fold up to put under a hot saucepan or even, dare I say, use to extract a baking pan from the oven. And then there is the good tea towel, the one that's just for show.

When I was living in Toronto, I had to get roommates because the rents were ridiculous. The girl who roomed with me was lovely, but there was one problem. She kept using the good tea towel, you know, the one that's for show. It was white and black, in a 'Paris' motif, and it hung from a hook in a spot that was obviously chosen for its display properties. There was another tea towel, a plainer one, that was close to the stove and sink, and simply screamed out, "Take ME!" Yet my roommate kept using the good tea towel, until it was no longer 'good'. I would come back after a weekend at home to find it hanging all crumply and stained. I would wash it and then replace it, and put the other tea towel in a more convenient spot, but my roommate had a penchant for using the good tea towel and I didn't know what to do. Why didn't you just tell her, you ask? Because that would be the most ridiculous conversation in the world, like "Can you not use this tea towel? It's for show." How do you say that without coming off like some weird kitchen textiles fanatic?

And you'll notice that when I referenced Ken and Kate respecting the good tea towel, I said 'until recently'. Because not too long ago, this happened:

One summer afternoon, finally fed up with the appalling turn of events, I swept into the kitchen dramatically. Brandishing the textile in question, I addressed my wrath at the room's occupants, Ken, Kate, and her boyfriend, who were in the middle of a porch renovation lunch break. "THIS—" I pronounced with a violent flourish, "THIS is the GOOD TEA TOWEL! And just look at it! You have sullied it beyond redemption!" Naturally, I was met with protests:

"But it was hanging right there!"

"There was nothing else to dry our filthy hands on!"

"What's a good tea towel?!"

"No!" I exclaimed, putting up a hand to silence their futile defense. "It simply won't do." I reached into a drawer and pulled out another, brand new tea towel. "This is now the good tea towel. You will recognize it because it has glitter thread running through the pattern. It is not—and I repeat NOT—to be used."

And you may scoff at the good tea towel, and most likely you are, but here's a fact: Laura Secord didn't abandon her children and make her way alone through the forest to warn the British about an impending American attack just because she felt like going for a jog. No, she was sick to f*cking death of the U.S. soldiers using her good tea towel. It's true. We won the War of 1812 because of the good tea towel. Of course, when the soldiers left Laura's house, they also left behind that one fork—you know the one I mean. It doesn't match any of your other forks, you didn't buy it, and you have no idea where it came from, yet every time you reach into the cutlery drawer, it's the first one your hand grabs, until finally, in a fit of pique, you yell "Stupid fork, I hate you!" and you throw it in the garbage. I may or may not have done this recently as I contemplated additional worst-case scenarios brought about by a new round of home renovations involving our upper porch, the one that I always assumed I'd use in case of fire:

Me: I need a new go bag. I don't think the one I have is big enough now.
Ken: Go bag?

Me: In case of fire. I have a bag, and a list of things to put in it, like the external hard drives, jewelry, the box of special notes and cards, my mother's watch...

Ken: The good tea towel.

Me: Obviously. But I think I need a new bag. There are a lot of things to take.

Ken: I'm assuming that in this scenario, Kate, the dog, and I are out of the house and safe.

Me: Of course. You're more important than any stuff. But once you're out, I'll run to the back bedroom, kick out the window, and throw the go bag and all my Paris paintings onto the balcony then climb down off the side porch.

Ken: Porch? Your plan would be perfect, except you've apparently forgotten that we currently don't have a side porch.

Me: WHAT? F*ck.

Ken: You could always go out the window by the stairs and leap from the front porch to the spruce tree.

Me: I'm not A LEMUR, KEN.

And now I not only needed a new go bag but a new fire plan to go with it. Ken suggested that I could tie a rope to one of the brackets in the brick and shimmy/rappel down to the ground, and I was like "How am I supposed to do that carrying a bag and several paintings, KEN?" Luckily, the porch reno finished without any major calamity and Ken, Kate, and her boyfriend managed to do all the work without using the good tea towel.

I also suffer from what I call "Straight Line OCD" or what experts call "an Extreme Need for Symmetry and Exactness" and it gets worse when I'm stressed out. Do you have any idea what kind of torture it is to simultaneously have an extreme need for symmetry and exactness as well as a house full of rugs that are constantly out of place? Why don't you get rid of the rugs, you ask? Because it's an old house with pine floors, and we need the rugs to stop the floors from getting damaged, muffle the creaking of the floorboards, and stop our feet from getting cold. Plus, when they're nicely centered on the floor, they're very beautiful. Why don't you get those rug gripper things, you ask? I have them under every damn rug and they don't work!

But I don't blame the rugs. I mean, it's not like they're deliberately askew-ing themselves. No, I blame Ken, who walks on them constantly, and especially the dog, who likes to run through a room at top speed, sliding on them and misaligning them. So I literally spend all my time straightening rugs. And if, right now, you're like "Why don't you just leave them? Who cares if they're on a weird angle?", IT MUST BE NICE TO BE YOU.

I feel bad for the dog though. His favourite game is something we call "Boogedy Boogedy" wherein he has a toy, and I pretend I want it, so I chase him around the kitchen island and then suddenly change direction, confronting him as I yell Boogedy Boogedy, then he takes off into the family room. There are, unfortunately, four rugs involved in this scenario.

The Dog: Ma! Do you want my toy?

Me: I most certainly do. I'm gonna get you and when I do, I'm gonna eat you!

The Dog (running): Hee hee!

Me: Boogedy boogedy!

The Dog: Wheeee—wait…why are you stopping?

Me: I have to straighten the rug.

The Dog: Are we done playing? 'Cause I'm just going to mess it up again.

Me: I know.

The most exhausting part of the game isn't running after the dog—it's having to constantly stop to straighten the rugs.

Not long ago, I bought a rug, a really beautiful Persian rug and I was supposed to pick it up but when I got to the guy's house, it wasn't where he said it would be, which was rolled up in a bag behind his garage. I messaged him and he was confounded. "I put four rugs out, each in their own bag, labelled with people's names," he said. Later, he messaged me that he'd looked at the security camera footage and saw that someone else had taken ALL rugs, instead of just the one they bought. And I was like "Oh, that's OK, and also I wasn't dancing while I was waiting at your door, I was jumping up and down from the cold." (Narrator's Voice: She was indeed dancing, having been unaware that there were, indeed, security cameras.)

But then that Friday, he messaged me that he'd gotten the rug back, so what choice did I have? So yes, another rug to straighten. But between that and chasing the dog, I'm staying in shape and no matter what angle you look at it from, that's a good thing.

Speaking of obsession, I do have a guilty secret. Well, I actually have more than one, but this is the only one I'm willing to share online, at least currently. I have, in the past, made certain revelations on my website about things I've done that hitherto had been unknown to my family, like the time I buried Ken's slippers in the garden in retaliation for his refusal to move them from the basement stairs (they were a TRIPPING HAZARD, KEN), or my attempt to put Kate's beta fish, suffering from beta bloat disease, out of its misery by pouring a bottle of absinthe into its tank:

Kate: You killed my fish and I find out ON YOUR BLOG?!
Me: He was really sick! I didn't want him to suffer. Besides, I told you about it at the time.
Kate: I was five! What else have you murdered?

But this time I'm not destroying anyone's blissful ignorance. No, this secret is more like a guilty pleasure, and it's the fact that I'm obsessed with the show *Hoarders*. You know the one I mean—a group of "hoarding experts and organizers" descend upon the home of someone who has been deemed a hoarder in order to simultaneously cure them of their disorder and make their house livable again. There are thirteen seasons of this American show, but because I'm Canadian, I can only watch when the American specialty channels are having a free preview month. But even then, it's all just the early seasons of rerun—I can easily recite right along with one of the…are they contestants?... participants?..: "I wouldn't classify myself as a hoarder; I would consider myself more of a saver, a rescuer of things", and then I yell back at the TV screen, "Nobody wants your garbage bag of dirty diapers, LINDA!" So a few months ago, in a fit of both pique at having to watch the same Wife Swap commercial for the one thousandth time on Paramount (leave the goddamn cat alone, KEISHA!), I broke down and bought Season 13 of *Hoarders* on Apple TV. And I was in my glory.

But why do you watch *Hoarders*? I hear you asking. A) Don't you have OCD? B) Isn't this show extremely stressful for you? And the answer to those questions is A) Yes, I do and B) No, it's not. Because the best part about Hoarders is at the end, when they get rid of all the stuff, clean the house, and then present it to the hoarder, who goes through and cries about how beautiful and spacious it is. And the rugs are all symmetrical and the table is set with all the corners perfectly perpendicular, and it's such an amazing payoff at the end. It's almost enough to make me want to become a professional organizer myself. But the thing about Season 13, and the reason I know I'd be terrible for someone who has hoarding disorder, is that Season 13 features several people who've hoarded some very nice things, unlike the mounds of trash, dirty diapers, dead animals, and moldy clothing that have been the mainstay of other seasons. I lay there night after night, watching antiques and paintings going into dumpsters and it's awful. Can you just imagine me, with my antique fetish and innumerable clocks that don't work, trying to help someone with hoarding disorder?

Dr. Zasio: Okay Diane, I'm so happy to see you letting go of all this furniture.

Me (whispers): That's a mid-century Eames chair, Diane. I'd keep that if I were you. And why are you throwing away all those picture frames? Put some chalk paint on those bad boys and frame old quilt squares with them—ooh, a mantle clock!!
Diane: I want all my sh*t back!!

Yep, I'd be awful at any job that required me to watch perfectly good stuff go into a junk truck. In fact, big junk day is where I GET my perfectly good stuff. But then again, I'm highly motivated to get things, fix them up, and actually resell them because if I don't, I get accused of being a hoarder myself:

Ken: Another clock? You're a hoarder!
Me: It's a really nice clock. Besides, I'd only be a hoarder if I had a closet full of broken clocks that I never looked at but couldn't bring myself to throw away. Speaking of closets full of crap you never look at and won't throw away, how's the closet in your office? Still full of magazines from 1988?
Ken: I just found this really nice clock online that you might like!

I guess there's a fine line between being a collector and being a hoarder.

WHAT ANY NORMAL PERSON WOULD DO

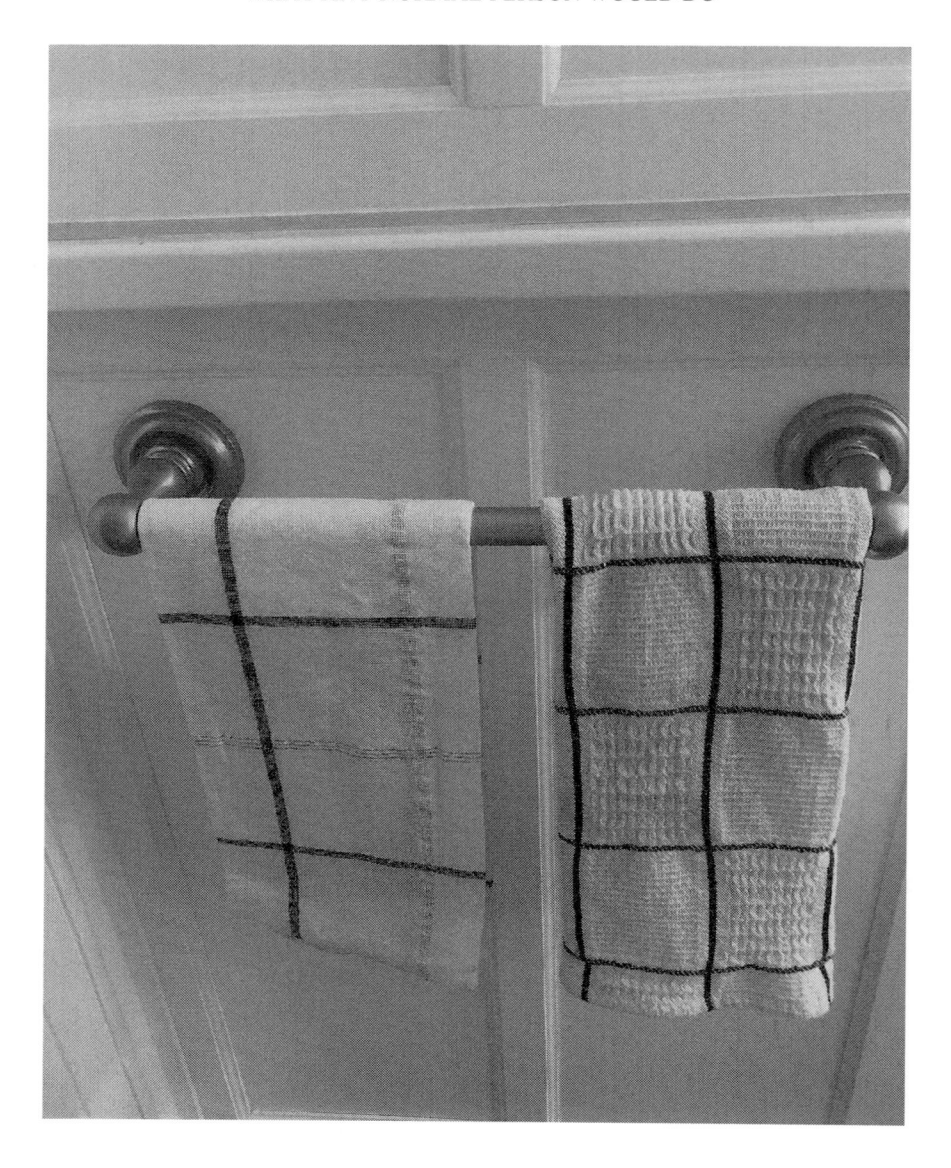

CHAPTER 8: WEIRD SIGNS, SAYINGS, AND WHATNOT

One of my favourite TV shows to binge-watch is a show called Elementary, a modern-day Sherlock Holmes series. The dialogue is very witty at times, and during one episode, Sherlock, played by Johnny Lee Miller, who is very awesome, says to Watson, played by Lucy Liu, "Opinions are like ani, Watson—everybody has one". It took me a second, then I figured out what he meant and it became my new favourite phrase. My previous favourite phrase was "This is not my circus; these are not my monkeys," which I would say to myself whenever the case called for it, which was fairly often.

But my new favourite phrase can also be used for a variety of occasions, and sounds pretty innocent until you look up what "ani" means (it's pronounced ayne-eye, by the way). When I started writing this, I looked up the spelling because I didn't know if it had one or two n's in it, and I discovered another interesting fact, thanks to dictionary.com, that while it means the plural of "anus", the word "anuses" is more commonly used. Really, dictionary.com? Because I've never in all my life had the need to refer to more than one anus, so whoever is making either of those words usage common is beyond me.

Maybe people who work at hemorrhoid cream factories. Or proctologists.

Then I thought about something similar that happened when I was teaching (absolutely NOT involving the word "ani"), when I remarked that someone had used two different mediums in their artwork, and one of my students, in the way that only teenagers can do, corrected me and said I should have said "medi-ahhh", because that was the plural of medi-ummm. So I did what all great teachers do when they're caught making a mistake, which is to totally make something up on the spot, and I told the kids with absolute confidence that when you are using a specific number in front of a word like that, you use the singular noun form, not the plural, because it was Latin. And nobody questioned it.

But I do get questioned a lot about some of the sayings that I regularly use that no one else seems to understand. I was talking once with some colleagues about the similarities between two pieces of writing that we were looking at. I happened to remark, "It's probably just a coincidence—you know, a million monkeys and a million typewriters, right?" Everyone looked puzzled and a little confused, so I clarified—"If you give a million monkeys each a typewriter….?" In retrospect, this was NOT a clarification, and everyone continued to look at me with confusion. I tried again.

Me: If you give a million monkeys a million typewriters, eventually one of them will write the bible. You've heard that saying before, right?

Colleague: Why would a monkey write a bible?

Me: No, it's a saying. It's the idea that random events can happen if you have enough time—and monkeys. So eventually, after hammering away, one of the monkeys might just randomly hit the right keys to recreate the words in the bible…sorry, it's just a saying. I'm not implying that the person who wrote this, or the bible, is a monkey…

At that point, I started to get panicky, because I wanted my colleagues to think that I was at least a little bit mentally competent, and I was starting to sound kind of like a crazy monkey-lady, which is like a crazy cat-lady, but with monkeys. Obviously. Then it occurred to me that I have a lot of strange sayings that I expect other people to understand, but a lot of the time (I've come to realize) they DON'T, because I've inherited a lot of my weird sayings from my family, over the course of many years, and they're fairly specific to a very small town in Scotland. Here are a few of my favourites, and I'll be honest—even I'm not sure exactly what they mean.

"If 'ifs' and 'ands' were pots and pans, there'd be no need for tinkers."

I have, after many years, interpreted this to mean that if you go to the kitchenware store a lot, you put pot/pan-repair people out of business. This saying has numerous applications because it sounds very clever, and it makes people think twice before they wish they had more pots.

"If hell was in Yoker, you'd get over for a penny."

Where the hell IS Yoker? Plus, I would think that going to hell wouldn't cost a measly penny—it would cost your ETERNAL SOUL. That one, I don't even begin to understand. My dad knows what it means, mostly because I think he made it up. Or one of his Scottish ancestors did, when they were drunk on Scotch at a bar in Yoker.

"You're such a dog in the manger."

This is a very unusual saying, and I don't know where it comes from, but it refers to a dog that doesn't really want to be in the manger (which is like a cattle stall), but he stays in there only because he doesn't want the cow to enjoy the manger. Ken grew up on a dairy farm, so I imagine this happened a lot, with people constantly chasing dogs out of cattle stalls. In human terms, this would be like a person who has called dibs on the long spot on the sectional couch, then won't give it up to someone else, even if they're really uncomfortable after watching the first 5 episodes of "The Walking Dead." Of course, I would NEVER do that.

"If wishes were horses, beggars would ride."

No, they wouldn't. From what I've seen of the local panhandlers who lived in my Toronto neighbourhood, if wishes were horses, beggars would sell them for a hot meal and a warm bed. What would a panhandler do in downtown Toronto with a horse? First, they would have to feed their horses, and most of them don't have enough money to feed themselves. This would most likely result in people sitting on sidewalks with signs that said, "Help me feed my horse." Would you feel sorry for someone with a sign like that? My favourite homeless guy, who would sit outside of Loblaws, had an adorable little terrier named Onyx, but he was smart enough to keep a bag of dog treats next to his sleeping bag as a way to engage people. When someone said, "What a cute dog," he asked if they would like to give Onyx a treat. Then people felt so sorry that Onyx was homeless too that they gave him money to help feed the dog. And it worked. Over a two-week span, I must have given him at least 10 dollars, and one day he remarked that he had just run out of treats for Onyx, so I bought him a bag when I went into Loblaws. He was very grateful and blessed me, which was nice. I can't see that happening with a horse though. I definitely wouldn't buy a bag of apples for a homeless guy's horse. Even if he was my favourite panhandler like Francis (that's not actually his name, but it's what I call him in my head). He just sat wrapped in a sleeping bag, with a ball cap in front of him, smiling at everyone and saying "hello" in a very pleasant way that made you WANT to give him money. I'll bet if he had one wish, it wouldn't be for a horse, it would be for world peace, because that's the kind of guy Francis was. I think.

"What you lose on the roundabout, you save on the swings."

I love this saying. It basically means the same as "6 of one, half a dozen of the other", so essentially, everything balances out. But it makes me think of carnivals, and that puts me in a festive mood. Of course, it could also refer to people with inner ear disorders, like Ken. Once, we went to a carnival and I convinced him to go on the Tilt-A-Whirl. So we paid "for the roundabout". Then he got so sick and dizzy that he couldn't go on any more rides. I had to half-carry him home because he could barely walk. Except we didn't really "save on the swings" because we had already bought tickets for some other rides, and ended up giving them away to random people because Ken was like, "Ooh, I felt like throwing up. Ooh, please take me home." So technically, we lost on the roundabout AND the swings because Ken was a big baby. A big, nauseated baby.

I asked Kate what kind of sayings I use that she thinks are weird, and this was the conversation:

Kate: Well, you say the F word a lot.
Me: That's not a saying, that's a swear word.
Kate: But I tell my friends, "Like my mom always says, 'F*ck.'"
Me (*laughs hysterically*)

When she read this, she got upset and said I was making her sound like she talked with an English accent. I don't know how that's even possible, but I encourage all of you to imagine that she DID say all that with an English accent, just to further enrage her.

I also quite often think about weird shit—for example:

Roadkill

Sometimes when I see roadkill, it makes me wonder—exactly how far past the "best before date" does a piece of roadkill have to be before the vultures won't eat it? When they're like "Ooh, that raccoon smells a bit dodgy—better give it a pass, Frank." Can vultures GET food poisoning, or is that just their job—to eat what no one else can, like nature's garburator? I don't know what it is about vultures, but they creep me out, especially the way you can always tell if there's something about to die in a field because the vultures are circling, like harbingers of doom. I once saw a vulture fly into an opening in the top of someone's barn, and all I could think was if it was my barn, I would leave in the night without any belongings, because the vultures were trying to tell me something.

Animal Zoos

Why would anyone put up a sign advertising an "Animal Zoo"? I saw this sign the other day, and my first thought was "As opposed to what?" What other kind of zoo is there? An insect zoo? Is it to differentiate itself from a Petting Zoo, letting people know that these animals are NOT the type you would want to pet? Like vultures? Anyway, I looked up the definition of 'zoo', and it can also be this: "a situation characterized by confusion and disorder". So maybe the sign was a warning. I envisioned people running around a small rural property, bumping into each other, swearing, acting all crazy, no one knowing what was going on. Now that's a zoo I'd pay money to see, even if it DOES sound just like a shopping mall on Black Friday.

Signs

The other day, I was in the Bay, a large department store, and I had to use the ladies' room. As I was leaving, I noticed a sign on the door that read, "All criminal activity in this bathroom is closely monitored." I stared at it for a minute or two, trying to figure out exactly what it meant. First, what KIND of activity are we talking about here? The only people I've EVER seen in that bathroom are elderly ladies. I mean, the Bay is not exactly Forever 21. Could there be a gang of old toughs who frequently gather in said bathroom to fence their stolen Hudson's Bay blankets and Estee Lauder cosmetics? And what does "closely monitored" mean? Are there security guards looking at hidden cameras whose reaction to every criminal transaction is "Huh. Take a look at that. Interesting. We'd better keep monitoring this. CLOSELY."

Another interesting sign that Ken and I saw a while back was one of those mobile signs at the side of the road, and it read, "Jesus said, 'The only way to my Father is through me.'" My first reaction was this:

Me: Did you see that sign? I don't believe Jesus said that.
Ken: Whuh? Why not?
Me: Well, don't you think it sounds a little arrogant? Like, UPPITY? I never think of Jesus like that. You've read the bible. Did Jesus really say that?

Ken: I don't remember.

Me: No. From what I know about Jesus, he would have said something more like, "It would be really nice and just super if you could let me help you find your way to my Father". Something non-aggressive, you know. That sign makes it seem like there's going to be a bar fight, and Jesus is all like, "You'll have to get through me to get to HIM!" Like Liam Neeson or something.

Ken: OK…

Me: Or John Wick—ooh! Like John Wick 5: The Resurrection!

Ken: You really don't know much about the bible, do you?

Me: I saw Jesus Christ: Superstar. I could totally picture John Wick as Jesus kicking over those moneylending tables in the temple then pulling out a machine gun--

Ken: That's not what happened.

Me: But in John Wick 5: The Resurrection, it would be a flea market where unscrupulous grifters were selling hoarded toilet paper and hand sanitizer for outrageous prices.

Ken: I'd watch that.

I saw one of my favourite signs from a few years ago, outside a church, which said, "Take Jesus on vacation with you". Ken and I were planning to take Kate to Great Wolf Lodge, this big waterpark, and I went into this reverie about what would happen if you literally COULD take Jesus on vacation with you to the waterpark. Would you have to stop him from trying to baptize the kids in the wave pool? Would all the water in the park automatically become Holy Water?

Would he get annoyed if strangers kept splashing him? Would he be like, "Okay, I'll go down the waterslide as long as I don't get my hair wet?" (Because that's what I always say.) Would he multi-task, and deliver a quick sermon while he was on the white-water raft with a bunch of other people? At the end of the day, I could picture him in a lounge chair, surrounded by small children, telling them parables until it was time for Pizza Hut and Pay-Per-View. At any rate, it would be a hell of a lot better than taking Satan on vacation to the waterpark with you. He'd be "that guy", you know, the one who always does the cannonballs into the pool, gets everyone in a 20-foot radius soaking wet, and laughs like he thinks he's so cool. He'd hog the Jacuzzi, make all the water boil, then force everyone to take Oil of Oregano. No wonder Satan never gets asked to go anywhere.

  But I love road signs. Some of them are so random. Like the sign not too far from where we live that says, "Don't B!tch About The Farmer With Your Mouth Full!" and underneath it asks, "What's Your Contribution?" Now, none of this makes any sense at all. First, you can't b*tch about ANYTHING with your mouth full. If you try, no one can understand what you're saying and then they get mad at you for spitting potato or chicken at them. Swallow first; complain later. That should be the motto of all whiny people. Second, I'm 57 years old and I've LITERALLY NEVER heard anyone complain about 'the farmer'. Like who's going around saying, "Those goddamn farmers and their CROPS. They should be ashamed of the way they make sure we get calcium from their UNHOLY MILK". Where did the animosity on this sign come from?! Is it, like, one disgruntled farmer fed up with being kept down by 'the man'?

> **The Man:** Hey Farmer Bob, your combine is blocking my driveway again. Would you mind moving it?
> **Farmer Bob:** DON'T B!TCH ABOUT THE FARMER, DAN.
> **The Man:** I wasn't b*tching, I just—
> **Farmer Bob:** IS YOUR MOUTH FULL, DAN?
> **The Man:** What? No, I only—
> **Farmer Bob:** I WILL MAKE A SIGN. WHAT'S YOUR CONTRIBUTION, DAN?
> **The Man:** I'm not giving you any money for a sign; I need you to move your combine.
> **Farmer Bob:** TYPICAL OF THE MAN.

The most ironic thing about this sign is that it's not on a farmer's field—it's actually next to a railroad bridge in a swamp, so I guess Farmer Bob has bigger worries than Dan The Man. (For the record, Ken grew up on a dairy farm, and I love farmers, obviously, and if anyone ever b*tched about them in my presence, I would set them straight.)

And then there was the sign in a small town we regularly go through that had two words on it: Landfill Cenotaph. There was a single arrow pointing down a side road. So the cenotaph is in a landfill? Or is it a memorial TO a landfill? Either way, that's not very respectful to our veterans, and it makes Remembrance Day ceremonies awkward:

MC: Let's have a moment of silence in remembrance of all of those who fought—hey! Can you turn off the bulldozers for one hot second?! Jeesh!

One of my favourite signs is one advertising a garden centre near where we live. It says, 'Gardening With An Attitude.'

Gardening with Attitude? Do drag queens work there? Surly teens, perhaps? All I could think of was this:

Customer: Hi, I'd like to buy a shrubbery. One that looks nice, and not too expensive.
Garden Centre Worker: F*ck off!
Customer: Wow, that's some attitude you have there.

And of course the best sign of all time…Who do you call if you have a noisy bath fan? The guy who plastered the signs saying, "I fix noisy bath fans" at every intersection in the city, obviously. Talk about a niche market—I can picture the high school Careers class with the teacher asking everyone, "So what do you want to do when you get out of high school?" and the one guy just lighting up: "I want to fix noisy bathroom fans!" and the teacher saying, "Amazing—there's a school JUST for that! It's called Hogwarts!" (I don't know why I thought of Hogwarts, but it made me laugh so hard picturing this guy at a school for magic and wizardry pointing his wand and yelling 'Reparo' at bathroom fans. Also, his name in this strange divergency is 'Tim' as in the following conversation:

Dumbledore: Hmm. My bathroom fan seems to be on the fritz. Someone get Tim—he's the best at repairing noisy bathroom fans.

Tim: Reparo!

Dumbledore: Thank you, Tim. Have a lemon drop.)

CHAPTER 9: RELATIONSHIPS

When we're driving in the car together, Ken and I often have fascinating conversations about the things we see. I like talking to Ken more than pretty much anyone I know, because we can talk about anything with complete seriousness. Like this:

Ken: Did you see the barn we just passed? There's a big sign on it that says, "Smoke Barn". I wonder why.

Me: You mean "Why is it a Smoke Barn?" or "Why label it?" Because to answer the first question, most likely because things get smoked in it, tobacco leaves for instance. Or maybe it's where people who work on the farm are allowed to smoke.

Ken: No, I mean why put a sign on it? If it's YOUR Smoke Barn, why tell other people about it?

Me: Maybe the owner is really proud of it and wants people to know that he finally reached his goal of owning a Smoke Barn.

Ken: It just seems weird.

Me: Maybe it's a liability thing, like for insurance. In case someone breaks into the barn, gets overcome by the smoke

and dies, their family can't sue you because you warned people that it was a Smoke Barn.

Ken: I think that if you break into a Smoke Barn and die, it was pretty much your own fault.

Me: I don't know about that—I remember hearing about a robber who was on the roof of a house trying to break in when he fell through the skylight and broke his back. He sued the owners for having a faulty skylight and won.

Ken: That's crazy.

Me: Maybe they should have put a sign on it.

Or this:

Once, we were on the highway and we got passed by a truck, and the sign on the side said, 'Underground Investigations", which got me thinking—what kind of business is that exactly? Private detectives? Sewer inspectors? People who work at cemeteries making sure that the holes are dug properly (or that the people in the coffins are really dead)? A secret agency that looks into other secret organizations? (of course, if you do that, it's kind of stupid to advertise it on your truck). When we got home, I looked it up, and it turns out that it could also be a heavy metal band, or a TV reality show that follows the adventures of 4 plucky men who "follow clues to the source of hazardous liquids that flow into storm drains." And now I really can't decide which one I'd rather be—a rock star or a sewer detective—because both sound pretty cool, and there's not technically much to choose between them aside from the hazmat suit, but that could also be your trademark as a heavy metal band. I mean, there are bands that perform in clown costumes, and bands that perform dressed like space aliens, so why not orange jumpsuits and gasmasks, am I right?

But an even better choice is "bucket or truck?" which I asked Ken as we passed a road crew trimming trees along the highway using cherry pickers:

Me: Bucket or truck?

Ken: Huh?

Me: Would you rather be the guy in the bucket or the guy in the truck controlling the bucket?

Ken: The guy in the bucket controls the bucket. The guy in the truck just sits there hanging out. So I'm going to say "truck".

Me: The guy in the bucket gets to control the bucket?! I'm totally saying "bucket". I'd be up and down and swooping around—it would be fun.

Ken: You're just supposed to trim the trees.

Me: Seriously? F*ck that. That sounds boring and labour-intensive. I change my choice to "truck".

Ken: We can't both be in the truck.

Me: Fine. You go in the bucket then.

Ken: But I don't want to be in the bucket…

Me: Stop being a baby and get in the damned bucket.

Ken is also really good at ignoring my randomness. I have family members who get really frustrated when people (i.e. me) interrupt them to ask questions, or clarify a point, and they will sometimes just give up (i.e. scream "Oh for God's sake, never mind!"). Luckily, Ken is used to this, and has no storytelling ego. He will just patiently address my thoughts and questions, then get back to his story. For example:

Ken: ...and then we all went to the RARE Slit Barn—
Me: Is that a STRIP CLUB?!
Ken: No, it's a nature preserve funded by a charity called RARE. A slit barn has vertical slits in it for ventilation—
Me: Ha! It SOUNDS like an exclusive strip club, like "Then we all went to the Rare Slit Barn, had a drink and a lap dance...
Ken: So anyway, they had students there who were training as interpreters—
Me: What, like for sign language? Was everyone hearing impaired? I'd love to learn sign language...
Ken: No, NATURE interpreters. To teach other people about the nature preserve—
Me: That would ALSO be a great name for a strip club: The Nature Preserve...
Ken: It was incredible how professional the students were. Everyone learned a lot.
Me: Slit Barn. That's awesome.
Ken: Sigh.

Unfortunately, Ken is too good a listener sometimes:

WHAT ANY NORMAL PERSON WOULD DO

Ken: Hey, Pete just posted a picture of the commemorative stone he bought for the new Lions' Club Splashpad. It has the name on the pub engraved on it.

Me: Cool. Did we buy a commemorative stone?

Ken: Of course.

Me: Nice. What does ours say?

Ken: 'Slippery When Wet.'

Me: WHAT?! It does NOT!

Ken: That's what you said you wanted.

Me: I WAS KIDDING!

Ken: You were? Too late now.

Ken and I have been married so long that sometimes we don't have actual conversations. We just KNOW.

Me: That.

Ken: Yes.

Me: I know, right?

Ken: Uh huh.

The other night, we were driving home, and we passed a sh*tload of pylons:

Me: What?

Ken: Couldn't get a building permit.

Me: Parking lot then.

Ken: Mmm.
Me: That fire.
Ken: Yeah.

Sometimes though, Ken gets bored in the car and starts to drive me crazy:

Ken: What's this button for?
Me: It has a car, skid marks, and the word 'OFF'. What do YOU think it does? Use your imagination.
Ken: I don't know. If I push it, will the car start to skid?
Me: Do you think it's a good idea to try?
Ken: Ummm…
Me: It's to turn off the TRACTION CONTROL! It's winter—why would you EVER want to do that!!?? Don't touch it!
Ken: Oh. Okay. What's this button for?
Me: It has a picture of a child inside a lock. Take a guess.
Ken: To lock your kids inside the car?
Me (*sigh*): Yes, that's right. To lock Kate in the car. You know, you have the exact same button in YOUR car.
Ken: I don't know what it's for in my car either. What does THIS button do?
Me: I'm going to cut off your fingers if you don't stop touching things.

Luckily Ken and I have a lot in common, including the same

kind of irreverence about a lot of things, especially death. Once we went to a funeral, and on the drive there, we had a chance to discuss some of the things that we wanted the other to know about our "arrangements". I, of course, am insistent that I be kept in an above-ground mausoleum, which Ken will build, due to my fear of being buried alive. Ken, on the other hand, is quite content to be cremated, and told me that if he had some "lead time", he would even build his own casket, a la Oscar, a character from our favourite show Corner Gas, so that I could save some money. That's what I love about Ken—he's always thinking about me.

Anyway, we got to the funeral and it was appropriately solemn and sad, but then we went through the receiving line (which is REALLLY different from the ones they have at weddings) and we were left to pay our respects at the coffin. While we were standing there in contemplation, Ken turned to me, pointed at the casket and whispered, "Remember Oscar? Beautiful woodgrain here." I was taken aback and kind of guffawed/choked/snorted, and I think a giggle escaped from me, to my horror. Ken and I spent the next 60 seconds staring violently at the floral arrangements and trying not to look at each other. I think it's true that old saying about laughing in the face of death, although it should be more of a defiant laugh, and not something out of a sit-com. On the way home, we passed a graveyard, and some workers had a bonfire going (let's assume they were burning leaves), and Ken, in that wonderfully naïve way he has, asked me, "Are they cremating someone?" to which I replied, "WTF, Ken! They don't do that in the actual graveyard!"

A little while later, Ken said to me, "If you don't want to talk about this, it's okay, but I was thinking about the kind of things we'd want the other person to read at our funerals." I immediately said poetry, and he immediately said that if he had enough "lead time" (he seems pretty positive that his impending doom will be pre-ordained), that he would video his own eulogy. I reminded him that no one would want to listen to him pontificate about critical thinking skills and the education of our young, let alone want to fill in a "descriptive feedback card" at the end of the funeral, but he was determined.

At this point, I told him MY plan, which is to write a eulogy FOR him, full of swearing and the liberal use of the F word, and then I'd tell people that I'd begged him to be more polite, but he was like "F*ck that! It's my f*cking funeral, and I can say whatever the f*ck I want." Of course, Ken rarely swears in real life (unless he hits his thumb with a hammer—you wouldn't believe how often THAT happens), and people would be shocked by his foul language, but at the same time they would admire me for following through with his last wishes. This would be my revenge for his refusal to pay my kidnap ransom (according to Ken, if you pay the kidnappers, it only 'encourages' them to keep kidnapping, so he maintains that if I was ever abducted, he would just wait for me to drive them crazy enough that they'd return me).

If Ken was ever kidnapped, I'm sure he'd be fine because he's a pretty self-sufficient guy. He's really good at taking care of me, but he hardly ever needs my help. I can only remember three actual times that he asked me to help him, aside from steadying things he's trying to cut or hammer, holding one end of a measuring tape, or proofreading something for him. I mean the serious kind of help, like emergency help. Once, he was really sick, and asked me to make him pudding. Another time, he set himself on fire and needed my help to put him out. I knew he was really in trouble because he started screaming "Help me!" and rolling around on the floor. Turns out that he was leaning against the stove while he was boiling potatoes, his shirt touched the element, and up he went. Fortunately, he has this weird habit of always wearing two shirts—it was the only thing that saved him from being badly burned. When I got him put out, he just lay there panting, then said, "Thanks." When he got up, I saw the scorch marks on the wooden floor where he was rolling and realized that it could have been so much worse.

One summer, I thought we had another emergency situation. He decided to finally trim the door of the shed by the driveway. For years, I'd been asking him to do it, because the door would only open partway then get stuck. He kept saying, "Yeah, yeah," until the day when he wanted to put our new lifejackets away:

Me: What are you going to do now?
Ken: I need to put the lifejackets away, which means I have to open the shed door, which means I have to take the door off the shed and trim it so it will open.
Me: Great thought process. I'll watch from the balcony.

So I watched him do it, since it didn't seem like a task for two.

I was sitting on the balcony half-watching and drinking a glass of wine, when suddenly I heard a slam, and Ken yelling, "Help!! I'm locked in the shed!!"

Apparently, the shed was on a bit of a lean, and now that the door wasn't stuck on the decking anymore, the weight of it caused it to swing shut. On Ken. I yelled back, "Don't worry! I'm coming!" but the problem was, he couldn't hear me, being locked in the shed and all, and I was upstairs on the balcony, probably the furthest point in the house from the shed. I started to make my way downstairs and the whole time, I could hear him pounding on the walls. I started getting all panicky and teary at the thought of my beloved husband there in the dark, not knowing if he was going to be rescued any time soon, possibly starting to suffocate. I kept yelling, "I'm coming!!" but the hammering continued. When I finally got to the shed and opened the door, there he was. He turned and smiled at me.

"I was so worried," I said. "I could hear you pounding the walls—I'm sorry I couldn't get here faster."

"Pounding the walls?" he said. "No, I figured you'd come eventually. I was just putting up some hooks for the lifejackets. That's why I was hammering. I'm just about finished—just prop open the door for me for a second so I don't get locked in again."

The most recent time that Ken needed my help was last fall when I was supposed to do a live author reading in another town. I get very stressed about things like this—not because of the reading, but because the venue was downtown with very little parking, and I have a lot of anxiety over parking. It's always my first question: "Where will we park?" In fact, I will actively avoid doing things if the parking situation is unknown or sketchy. I'm acquainted with some people who are about to open a new store and my first reaction was, "No one will ever go there. It's right downtown and the parking is terrible." By 'no one', I obviously meant me, because I know I'm the only weirdo who stresses about parking and most people are happy to just leave their cars literally anywhere:

Carefree Person 1: Oh my, we're two miles from the venue. Stop the car. Right here.
Carefree Person 2: Excellent choice. I shall abandon the vehicle on this verge.
Carefree Person 1: It's a lovely night for a trek to the concert and the weather continues charming. Well, it's raining slightly, but no matter.
Carefree Person 2: Might we be late? Yes. Yet it matters not.

So anyway, I said to Ken, "We need to leave by 2:15 at the latest, so make sure you're ready to go. I'm serious." And Ken nodded and went back outside to 'finish up the one thing he was doing', which was using the table saw to make a small wooden box to house the transformer that runs our outdoor Christmas lights. I was preparing by silently reading and timing myself in the kitchen when he came back in, around a quarter to two. He looked weird.

Me: What's wrong? Why are you cradling your hand…

Ken: I think I've really hurt myself.

Me (panic rising): What did you do?

Ken: I cut my finger. With the table saw.

Me: Let me see!...Oh god. We're going to the hospital.

Ken (weakly): No, it's okay. I'll just tape it.

Me: You can't tape THAT. You need stitches.

Then Kate came in:

Kate: What's going on? Let me see. JESUS! Is that bone?

Ken: Can you stitch it up? You're a vet tech.

Kate: NO! Go to the hospital.

In the meantime, I was calling to cancel my reading, and then calling the nearest Urgent Care to see if they did stitches, to which the nurse I spoke to cheerfully replied, "We sure do!" as if people almost dismembered themselves all the time. Which, in fact, people probably do, judging by the casual attitude when we arrived, Ken holding a wad of blood-soaked paper towels around his hand and me looking like I was about to faint, cry, or both. The nurse was like, "Go sit down in the waiting area, and someone will bring you gauze."

After about an hour, we finally saw the doctor (which was actually pretty quick, although I think we maybe got pushed to the head of the line due to ALL THE BLOOD), and his immediate and unsurprising reaction was, "Wow, that needs stitches. But it doesn't look like you severed the ligament, which is a good thing, or you would have lost the use of the finger altogether."

Ken: I hope you can fix it. It's my favourite finger.
Doctor:
Me: It's the one he uses for texting. The ONLY one. That's why he texts so slowly. Will this heal quickly? Otherwise, I'll never hear from him.

After he was all stitched up, we came home. Did we have a conversation that started with "How many times have I TOLD you to wait until the blade stops" and ended with "I love you and I'm so happy it wasn't worse"? We definitely did.

Of course, one of the best things about Ken is that he is completely normal, even in my dreams. I'm a very vivid dreamer. I have crazy movie length dreams that are like watching crime dramas, and sometime horror movies. Last month, I was watching a dream unfold where a patient in a hospital was extremely ill, and detectives discovered that she had been given an injection of "lupus alcoholis" by a guy who was stalking her, and this had caused her to become deformed and almost die. The doctor at the hospital formulated an antidote, and the detectives arrested the stalker. It was awesome, and cheaper than actually going to the movies. This happens to me all the time, and it's wonderful and sometimes scary too, especially when the dreams involve Kate getting kidnapped or my mom driving a car into a river and me trying to rescue her (don't worry, Mom, I saved you)—stuff like that.

But for some reason, whenever I dream about Ken, it's always the most perfectly normal dream you could have. In fact, they're about as close to real life as you can get. Last night, I dreamed that Ken was driving me to work, but I forgot my cell phone so we were going back to get it, when he spotted a garage sale and pulled over. The only thing they were selling was these really expensive clock faces and Ken got super-excited, because he keeps talking about making his own clock (in real life, not in the dream). So I said to him (in the dream, not in real life), "Spending that kind of money on a clock face defeats the purpose of making your own clock." He looked disappointed, but he agreed with me, and we carried on back home to get my phone.

WTF kind of dream is that?! The only way it differed from real life is that Ken NEVER pulls over for garage sales unless I make him. In the future, I'm going to try a little "lucid" dreaming and introduce some zombies onto the field of play, just to see what he does. A minute ago, I asked him what he was doing, and he said "resting" (even though we both knew he was just in his Nothing Box), so in my head I was like, "Just see how tired you're going to be after a night of The Walking Dead. Ha ha, Ken!!"

Ken, like many men, has a Nothing Box. And that to me seems to be the main difference between most men and women. I heard once a long time ago on a talk show that men have a Nothing Box in their heads. So when you say to a man, "What are you thinking about?" and he says, "Nothing," he's telling you the truth. There is literally NOTHING in his mind because he's in the Nothing Box. And sometimes, I'll ask Ken a question, and I'll be waiting for the answer, and he seems to be taking a really long time thinking about it. Only he's not. He's still in the Nothing Box, and when I ask if he has an answer yet, he'll look at me kind of surprised, like he forgot we were in a conversation. This happens quite often when we're having a "debate", and I'll ask, "What the hell is wrong with you?", totally expecting a response, because I'm not being rhetorical, but then he just goes into his Nothing Box when he's SUPPOSED to be figuring out the answer.

I don't have a Nothing Box. I never think about nothing. In fact, I can't even meditate—if you ask me to clear my mind, I immediately start thinking about how to do that, how long I should do it for, what does "empty' mean in this context anyway? And a thousand other things that ultimately prevent my mind from actually emptying. Ken, like most men when told to empty their minds, are just like "Done. Let's meditate." Then they go into the Nothing Box and stay there for a while. It's like the saying "Lost in thought". When a man is lost in thought, it's just ONE thought that he's contemplating, like shortcuts or compass points or sandwiches. When a woman is lost in thought, she is literally lost in a maze of bizarre and random ideas that jump from one thing to another like a hyperactive frog, but the one thing she is ALWAYS doing is problem-solving and making decisions. Even if it's not readily apparent to the guy in his Nothing Box.

Ken is not good at the decision-making process. Oh, he can MAKE decisions all right, but then he pretends that he needs my help to figure out things, which is super-frustrating. We have had MANY debates over the years about why he does this—here are three examples of this little quirk of his:

Me: Let's go for a walk.
Ken: Sure. Which way do you want to go?
Me: Towards the park would be good.
Ken: No, we should go towards the store so we can check our lottery ticket.

Me: Which one of these paint chips do you like best?
Ken: I don't care. They're both fine.
Me: I like this one the best.
Ken: No, that one's too yellow-y. The other one is the colour we should paint the room.

Ken: Should we check into the hotel first or return the rental car?
Me: Return the car.
Ken: No...blah blah obscure reasoning...
Me: WTF KEN?!

I always say, "Why did you ask for my opinion if you already knew what you wanted to do?!" Then I wait for an answer. But I never get one, because he's in his Nothing Box. Lucky bastard.

It's an unwritten rule (or maybe it's written down somewhere, like in the bible or People Magazine) that it's perfectly acceptable for a married woman or man to have a celebrity husband/wife. AND a celebrity boyfriend/girlfriend. Isn't that like extra cheating, you ask?

You're already married, then you get to have a pretend husband, then you pretend-cheat on BOTH of them with a pretend boyfriend?! Well, yes. But it's okay, because it's not like I'm EVER going to meet Idris Elba (husband) or Benedict Cumberbatch (boyfriend).

Once I saw a link for a Playbuzz quiz that said it could tell me who my REAL celebrity boyfriend was, so I took it. There were only 5 questions, one of which was "Blonde or Brunette"? So the field was pretty open, apparently. After I answered "Brunette", the little swirly thing swirled and then it came up with Zac Efron. No, Playbuzz—just NO. If anything, Zac Efron would be my celebrity CHILD. And that would be cool. I'll bet Zac would read everything I wrote and say, "Hey Pretend-Mom, you are SO funny!"

But there's a lot of competition out there for celebrity spouses. One day at lunch, a bunch of us from work were discussing upcoming movies and other things, and I said I was totally pumped to see *The Dark Tower*, based on Stephen King's novels and starring Idris Elba, so like two of my absolute favourite things all rolled into one. And then one of the women said, "Oh Idris Elba—he's my celebrity husband." And I was like, "No. NO. He's MY celebrity husband! He's been mine since I saw him in *Luther*." Then another woman countered with, "No, he's mine. He's been MY celebrity husband since *The Office*." I was chagrined because I didn't know that Idris Elba had even been on *The Office*, but I immediately offered to throw down with either of them. Then I took it back, because they're both really nice people, and I still have Benedict Cumberbatch all to myself. ISN'T THAT RIGHT, LADIES?

I told Ken all about this, and he was like, "Am I allowed to have a celebrity wife?" I told him of course he was.

Me: Who would be your celebrity wife then?
Ken: Ummm. I don't know.
Me: You can pick anyone. Who's a movie star that you really like?
Ken: I can't think of anyone.
Me: What about that woman who was in the movie we saw last night?
Ken: No. Oh wait—I'm going to say Nicole Karkic.
Me: Who the hell is Nicole Karkic?
Ken: She's on The Weather Channel. She's smart and she really knows her weather.
Me: You can't pick someone from The Weather Channel!
Ken: Why not? You said I could pick anyone. There's also that meteorologist on CTV News—she's very reliable.
Me: All right, then…

I guess I should consider myself lucky to be married to a man who appreciates a woman who's climate-savvy, instead of being all about her physical looks. Me, I also appreciate Benedict Cumberbatch's…intelligence.

Of course, as part of our relationship, we regularly compete, as most couples do, to see who can outdo each other on special occasions. For instance, on our 27th Anniversary. Ken said "Happy anniversary" first, but I was the first one to post it on Facebook, so I thought I won. Then he posted a picture of two puzzle pieces which said "You" and "Me", and I was like, "Aww—that's sweet!" But then I realized it was a gif, and when I watched it, the two little puzzle pieces moved towards each other and fit together. Which sounds really cute, but the one puzzle piece had a part like a very large phallus, and the other one had an opening, so when they fit together, it looked super-dirty. And then I also realized that the puzzle piece with the phallic bit said, "You", as in me, and the apparently-lady piece said, "Me", as in Ken, and that was even more disturbing in terms of what Ken intended:

Me: I think you got the genders on those puzzle pieces wrong. At least I'm hoping. I think we're both too old to be trying stuff like that.

Ken: What are you talking about?!

Me: That gif was a little dirty.

Ken: It was two puzzle pieces. What's dirty about THAT?

Me: Did you watch the animation? Very pornographic.

Ken: They fit together! It's cute, like "we're a perfect fit"! Get your mind out of the gutter.

Me: Super-dirty. What WILL our friends think?

Ken: Happy Anniversary, weirdo.

Me: Yeah. Ich liebe dich. That means "I love your--"

Ken: No, it doesn't.

WHAT ANY NORMAL PERSON WOULD DO

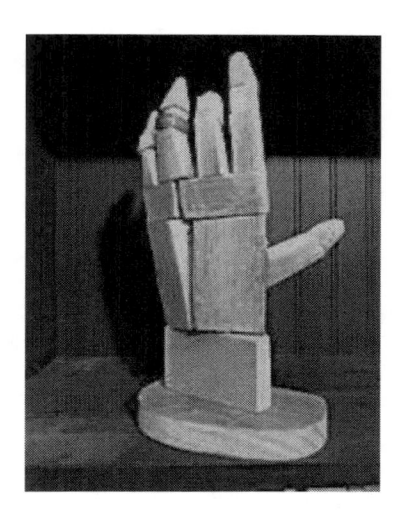

CHAPTER 10: I LIKE TO WATCH

(Although this chapter comes directly after Relationships, the one has nothing to do with the other, so get your mind out of the gutter.)

I'm a very visual person—I have a degree in English Literature as well as a degree in Film Studies. Which means I get to watch movies and TV whenever I want, without anyone being able to criticize me because IT'S MY FIELD. And being an expert on television and cinema leads to all sort of interesting observations:

Once Kate and I were in a car dealership waiting for them to install her snow tires. In the waiting lounge, there was a big screen TV, and since it was the middle of the afternoon, there was a soap opera on. I've never actually watched a soap opera, but I recognized it from the strange way it was filmed. Kate had never seen one either, and we weren't very interested at first, reading stuff on our phones, until suddenly Kate poked me and said, "What the hell is this crazy show?" I looked up and a man and woman were talking. She was fully made up with bright red lipstick and he looked like he'd been crying. Then the camera pulled back—they were both standing on the ledge of a building. I always thought soap operas were about romance and rich people, but this was really weird, so we started to watch on the grounds that it would be 'good for research purposes'. It was hard to pick up the storyline midstream but here's what we gleaned:

The girl on the ledge, or the guy, or both have been shot. She wants him to jump off the building with her for some unknown reason. She is wearing a hospital gown, and they both have matching bullet wounds. They argue then gaze into the distance. The camera cuts away.

A blonde woman is arguing with a doctor. He's been keeping secrets (about what, it's not clear), but the name Tony is mentioned. She's upset about Kiki being shot. Who the hell is Kiki? How is Tony involved? Did he shoot Kiki? They gaze into the distance. The camera cuts away.

Another blonde woman is talking to a man called Sonny. Her hands are covered in blood. He seems to be a gangster type—is she his wife? She's also upset about what happened to Kiki, and seems to be accusing him of having something to do with it, prompting Kate and me to ask each other, "What happened to Kiki? Do you know?!" Neither of us do. We all gaze into the distance. The camera cuts away.

An older man comes into the room where the first blonde woman is waiting. She slaps him across the face and tells him that none of this would have happened if he hadn't blackmailed her into…smuggling guns? Is he Tony? Did he shoot Kiki? In the foreground, a nurse with a heavy German accent says to a doctor, "Zere is someone on ze roof." They all gaze into the distance. The camera cuts away.

We're back on the roof. The girl and the guy are arguing more heatedly. Another man comes to the door and sees the guy. "Tony, what are you doing up there?" he asks. Finally, we know who Tony is. "Oh, Kiki, I can't live without you, and I can't live with what I've done to you," he replies, looking at the girl. "Who are you looking at?" asks the other guy. The camera pans back, the girl is gone, and Tony no longer has a bullet wound. Kate and I look at each other and gasp. The girl is a figment of his imagination! The other man backs through the door, leaving Tony alone on the ledge. Nice friend, that one. Maybe he shot Kiki and doesn't want Tony to know. Tony gazes into the distance. The camera cuts away.

The second blonde woman is now in a public bathroom. She finds a scrub brush and starts scrubbing the blood from her hands. Suddenly a really hot, half-naked man appears. Apparently, this is a MAGIC bathroom. They argue about doctor-patient confidentiality and he wraps her hands in bandages because she's scrubbed them raw. Did the blonde woman shoot Kiki? Could this be an homage to Lady Macbeth trying to scrub the guilt from her soul? Are the people who make soap operas really that well-read? We all gaze into the distance and the camera cuts away…

…to a police precinct where apparently only two woman work

because there is literally no other cop in the entire building. They are arguing. The older woman is begging the younger cop for a favour. "Just give me a few weeks," she says. "Then I'll tell you everything you need to know about Sonny, and Don, and Carlos, and Andy." Ok, we know who Sonny is, but who the hell are all these other guys? Suddenly the older man from the previous scene who blackmails people into gun smuggling appears. "Captain, what can I do for you?" says the female cop. Captain?! He's blackmailing people into arms dealing and HE'S the Captain of the police precinct? They argue and he tears up a warrant that she has for the first blonde woman. "I've given her immunity," says the Captain. For what? we wonder. Did SHE shoot Kiki? Because at one point, we were sure she was Kiki's mother. This is getting more confusing. They gaze into the distance. The camera cuts away.

We're back on the roof. The doctor from a previous scene is there, trying to talk Tony off the ledge. Suddenly Sonny appears. It turns out that he's Tony's father. He jumps up on the ledge with Tony and… offers to jump with him. Kate and I hope he's bluffing—we've grown quite fond of the both of them. More people arrive, and finally, Tony comes down off the ledge and into the arms of his gangster dad. The credits roll.

Kate and I look at each other. "So who the hell shot Kiki?" she asks. "Damned if I know," I reply. We gaze into the distance.

But as much as I enjoy watching television and movies, I also think I'd be great IN them.

1) Let's start with Star Wars, at the moment before the Death Star is about to be destroyed...

>**Obi-Wan:** Mydangblog, trust your feelings.
>
>**Me:** I really wish you would call me Player One.
>
>**Obi-Wan:** Concentrate, Mydangblog.
>
>**Me:** But all the other guys get cool nicknames! There's Red Leader, Gold Leader, Wedge, Goose…aw, Goose just got exploded.
>
>**Obi-Wan:** Goose was from Top Gun. Will you please concentrate?!
>
>**Me:** Ok, I'm going into the weird tunnel. I'm gonna blow sh*t up!
>
>**Obi-Wan:** Use the Force, Mydangblog.
>
>**Me:** No way. Imma use this visor thing with the targeting computer in it.
>
>**Obi-Wan:** LET GO!
>
>**Me:** Are you Force-splaining how to destroy a Death Star to me?
>
>**Darth Vader (heavy, pervy breathing):** The lunacy is strong with this one.
>
>**Obi-Wan:** Mydangblog, trust me.
>
>**Me:** That heavy-breathing perv just shot my robot! That's it!

Tick tock, m*therf*cker—your time is up! (*puts on theme song which is obviously Boom Boom Pow, blasts everything in sight with my laser guns, manages to hit portal, Death Star detonates*)

I know—it ends just like the real Star Wars, but it was a lot more fun.

2) The Empire Strikes Back

Scene: Out on some glacier.

> **Me:** Holy sh*t, it's cold.
> **Obi-Wan:** Mydangblog. Mydangblog.
> **Me:** You again? I told you to call me Player One.
> **Obi-Wan:** You will go to the Disco-Bar system and learn yoga.
> **Me:** What the actual f*ck? Urghhhh, it's so cold…
> **Han Solo:** Mydangblog!! Come on, give me a sign here! There's not much time! I'm going to cut open this Tauntaun and put you inside it to keep you warm.
> **Me:** GROSS. I'D RATHER DIE.

So in my world, I only appear in two Star Wars movies, but I stand by my choice. Tauntaun intestines are disgusting.

3) 2001: A Space Odyssey

Opening scene:

Monkeys all screaming and having some kind of monkey war. I suddenly appear, like a strange female monolith. They stop and stare.

> **Me:** Hey chimps! Which one of you wants to be my monkey butler?

(*One monkey tentatively walks forward. He picks up a big bone from like a Tyrannosaurus or whatnot, and advances on me.*)

> **Me:** OK, cool. I shall name you Ralph Van Wooster.

(*Monkey shakes his head and waves the bone menacingly. More monkeys start to move towards me.*)

> **Me:** I think I've misjudged this situation terribly.

(*Monkeys stop their in-fighting and attack me with their dinosaur bones. Then they, after having united against me, live in peace and harmony until the end of time.*)

4) Psycho

Shower Scene:

Me, in the bathtub, splashing around and having a dandy time. For some reason, the shower curtain is pulled closed, which I would NEVER do in real life because I need to know if someone is sneaking up on me, but let's suspend our disbelief for a moment. There's the silhouette of a figure approaching, knife raised. The shower curtain is suddenly pulled back. Violins screech and then stop abruptly. Norman Bates looks confused.

> **Norman:** Why aren't you in the SHOWER?!
> **Me:** Showers are the devil's cleaning system! Get out of my bathroom, you psycho! (*grabs hammer that I always keep on the bathtub ledge and breaks his kneecap as theme song, Boom Boom Pow, plays*)
> **Norman:** I wouldn't even harm a fly!...

Despite my illustrious acting career, I'm actually quite introverted, believe it or not, but I love to people-watch, just observing them doing random and interesting things. And while I'm sure if anyone watched ME, they'd come to the conclusion that I'm out of my mind, I also wonder the same about other people too, simply based on the weird things I've seen over the years, especially living in Toronto.

When I first moved into my condo, I was initially alarmed by how high up I was, and the fact that I had floor to ceiling windows made me a little dizzy. But I soon learned to love the view—I could see the sun rising over the lake in the morning, and the city lights were gorgeous at night. But the best part was that my condo directly overlooked the roof of the building next door, which, when I moved in, featured a quite lovely roof garden with raised boxes of shrubberies, lighted paths, benches, and so on. Then around the beginning of March, I looked out and saw a crew of workers who were starting to dismantle the whole thing. I was initially dismayed, but not long after they ripped it apart and took it down to bare concrete, they started laying down new rubber membrane and then patterned paving stones. I had ongoing hope that one day it would be an even more beautiful rooftop garden. But the PACE of the workers was starting to concern me. There were 4 men, and they arrived around 7 am every day, and they were gone by the time I got home from work. And so far, they hadn't even finished LAYING the paving stones. One Thursday night when I got in, it seemed that most of the stones at my end of the roof were in place. Except for one spot, where there was a hole with a single paving stone missing. I assumed they had left it because it was quitting time, and that it would be easy to finish up the next morning. Was I ever wrong.

On Friday morning, I got up, and the crew was there. They were too far away to really identify but there were 4 guys—let's call them Bill, Frank, Bob, and Monty. Over the course of the next hour, as I was getting ready for work, I was fascinated by their activity—or lack thereof:

7:02 – Bill, Frank, and Monty are wandering aimlessly around the roof. Bob comes out of the porta-potty. (I have NO idea how they got a porta-potty up there.) I go into the bathroom and wash my face.

7:05 – Bill is staring at the hole. Frank is leaning against the wall, having a smoke. I moisturize.

7:07 – Bill is standing IN the hole. Frank is staring at him. I wash my hair.

7:10 – Bill and Frank are BOTH standing in the hole. It's a tight fit AND they're facing each other. I dry my hair.

7:15 – Frank is standing in the hole. Bill is about 10 feet away, lying on his stomach facing the hole and using his thumb as a gauge. For what exactly, I have no idea. Monty is hovering nearby. No sign of Bob. I pour out some cereal and go back into the bathroom to put on some make-up.

7:20 – Frank is out of the hole, and Bill is once again in it. He's jumping up and down. Frank observes him carefully. I put my cereal bowl in the sink and apply mascara.

7:22 – Frank and Bill are kneeling on either side of the hole. They are facing each other and look like they are genuflecting. Perhaps a small god lives in the hole. I brush my teeth.

7:24 – Monty is standing in the hole. Frank and Bill observe him carefully. Could it be a time-travel portal? Maybe that explains what happened to Bob, whom I haven't seen in a little while. No, wait—Bob has just come out of the porta-potty again. So much for the time-travel theory. Unless the porta-potty IS the portal. Hmmm. I go into my room to get dressed.

7:29 – Monty and Bill are standing next to the hole. Bob has made his way over, and seems to be instructing Frank on how to kill an insect by stomping repeatedly on it with his foot. He stomps, then looks encouragingly at Frank, who then stomps a little himself. They continue this for several minutes. I pack my lunch.

7:33 – Bob and Frank are still "killing insects". Monty and Bill are now both lying on their stomachs across from each other, facing the hole, and both are using their thumbs as gauges. Again, for what, I have no idea. I get my bags ready to leave.

As I left for work, Bill was once again IN the hole. Monty, Frank, and Bob were observing him carefully. I had hoped that, based on the efforts of the morning, the hole would be filled by the time I got home from work.

When I arrived at my condo at the end of the day, I was anxious to see what progress the crew had made. Not only was the original hole still visible, there were now at least 14 other holes where once there were none. It was going to be a long summer.

But there are fun things to watch in my own neighborhood, especially since I have a balcony with a bird's eye view of any mysterious goings on. We live kitty-corner to two churches—I call them the "Platform Diving Jesus Church" and "The Other Church". As you may guess, I don't attend either of them. I got their names from the fact that a few years ago, the doors of the church directly across from us were painted with an angel on one side, and Jesus on the cross on the other, both in gold paint. It looks very nice up close but from far away, it looks like Jesus is about to dive off a cliff.

Anyway, from my bathroom window, I could see five men standing around a piano which was sitting on a flat cart on the church walkway. It looked like they had just unloaded it from a rather small mini-van—a feat unto itself, I would imagine. I could hear yelling, so I opened my balcony door. The men had surrounded the piano and were having a very loud discussion in what sounded like German. Were they an angry yet musical Saxon mob intent on a good sacking? After a few minutes though, it seemed like their intention was to put the piano INSIDE the church. And I say 'seemed' because they kept just wandering around the piano, staring at it dubiously, and talking a lot. I had nothing better to do, and it was a beautiful sunny morning, so I went out onto the balcony to watch.

After a lot more Germanic discussion, the youngest-looking guy ran over to the mini-van and brought out a long strap, which he looped around the piano. 'Here we go,' I thought. Nope. They all just stood back and stared at the piano again. I wanted to yell, "Just push the damn thing, for Christ's sake!" which seemed appropriately church-y, but then the guy ran back to the mini-van. He reappeared with what looked like a gas can and at first I thought maybe they were going to set the piano on fire and claim an angel spoke to them from within it, like a 'burning bush-type scenario', so that they could blame God for not getting it inside the church. However, it was only a toolkit. The young guy took out a hammer and started hammering at something while the rest just stood around. One of the other men put his hood up, like he didn't want to be recognized, and frankly I don't blame him because I was at the point where I just wanted to march over and push the piano through the doors myself. Then the one with the hammer ran back to the mini-van and grabbed what I thought was a blanket of some kind, but it was just his coat, which he randomly donned, then he looped a harness around his shoulders and waist.

'Aha!' I thought. 'He's going to hook himself to the piano and pull it in like a team of oxen' but again, I was disappointed. And then I was really confused because they started pushing the piano down the walkway and I had a moment where I thought they were going to take a run at the door with it, but again, NOPE. They wheeled it back towards the mini-van and I was like "What? Don't give up Hans, Karl, Kristoff, Otto, and Gunther!" (which is what I had affectionately started to call them in my head), but then they wheeled it PAST the mini-van and kept going. Down the street.

I watched until they were out of sight, then I quickly got dressed and hopped in the car to see where they went, but they, and the piano, had disappeared like some kind of biblical miracle. But then I had a terrible thought—what if I had just witnessed a crack German heist squad, not unlike the villains in *Die Hard*, actually ROBBING the church?! I'd have to wait until Christmas to find out when *Die Even Harder: Music To Your Ears* was released.

Of course, reality is better than television, unless you invent your own reality shows. I love reality shows. I've loved them ever since I was five years old and I was on a children's reality show called "Romper Room". It was one of the most popular shows on Ontario television, and it consisted of a different group of children each week just playing and doing activities under the supervision of a kindly, teacher-type lady. At the end of each show, Miss____ (there were several women who played the role—mine was Miss Grace) would hold up a magic mirror, and say, "I can see Johnny, and Sarah, and Ian, and…." Kids across the province would sit fixated, desperately hoping to hear their name. I don't know why my parents decided to put me on the show, but two incidents cemented for me the fact that reality shows have only a tenuous relationship with reality.

First, I kept jumping up and down, prompting the director to tell me to stop. "You're TOO excited," he said. But I was excited. A SUPER f*cking excited 5-year-old, and I had to stifle my real enthusiasm because it was TV. Second, they taped all five episodes for the week on one Saturday, and I kept getting into sh*t for contradicting Miss Grace when she would start the next segment with "What day is it today, boys and girls?" Everyone was supposed to say 'Tuesday' or whatever, but I yelled "Saturday!!" every time. Once again, the director had to talk to me about how we were only "pretending" and to just play along. Yep, that's me—a non-conformist pain-in-the-ass from an early age.

Lately, Ken and I have been consumed with watching reality shows. No, not reality shows like "The Bachelor" or "Big Brother", which we have never watched because, let's face it, even if you like those shows, you have to admit they're pretty dumb:

The Bachelor

Bachelor Guy: I was going to give you a rose, but then you ate sushi in a weird way.

Girl: I'm so sad now.

Big Brother

House Guy: I was going to save you, but then you ate all the sushi.

Girl: I didn't eat all the sushi. It was Bob! And he ate it in a weird way!

House Guy: Bob! I might have known. You are evicted!

And please bear in mind that I have NEVER watched either of these shows and just made the previous sh*t up based on what I've seen on Twitter. I have no idea if I'm even close.

Ken and I, however, have been watching these very avant-garde-y reality/competition shows. The first thing we really got into was "Forged in Fire", where 4 blacksmiths faced off against each other to create knives and daggers and swords and whatnot. In the first round, they had to make a weapon and then test them on stuff like dead fish and sheep carcasses. Then it was narrowed down to two finalists who went back to their "home forge" to create a super-weapon and isn't a HOME FORGE the most incredible thing that you could possibly have? Like, "Hey honey—I might be late for dinner because I'm making a giant f*cking sword in my HOME FORGE." Anyway, it was a very weird show, with a judge whose only job was to attack things with the contestants' blades and then say, very proudly like a happy dad, "Your blade will cut. Your blade will kill." But then we had to stop watching it when we found out that they specifically slaughtered animals to use them on the show, and that just seemed mean.

The most recent show we watched on Netflix was called "Blown Away" and it was a glassblowing competition, which might sound kind of tame, but BELIEVE ME, it was very awesome and also the glassblowers would get quite bitchy with each other. It started with 10 competitors and every episode there was a challenge, with one person "blowing the judges away" (I'm sure EVERYONE is glad the word 'away' is in there) and one person being sent home for being an utter disappointment. Spoiler Alert: I'm going to give away the ending so don't read this if you're planning on watching the whole first season. In the last episode, it came down to Janusz, a very experienced glassmaker who was very technical and talented, and Deborah, who wasn't quite as talented, but who talked a good game. They were tasked with filling a gallery space with something "immersive", whatever the f*ck that means. Janusz did a whole series of pieces on climate change and hope for the future, and Deborah made a giant fried egg, a frypan, and a bunch of very phallic sausages. The judges were struggling with the whole thing, but then Deborah cried and said that her piece represented the way she'd been marginalized her whole life and SHE WON. With BREAKFAST. And there was literally a petition on Change.org to award the $60 000 prize to Janusz, so you can tell how much people were into this show.

Which got me to thinking. If I could create a new reality show, what would it be? Here are a couple of thoughts. Also, for the purpose of this exercise, Alex Trebek is the host of every show, because even though he's dead, he's still the best host of everything and I love him.

Show 1: Tanked

This show is a fish tank decorating competition. Every week there's a new theme.

Alex Trebek: All right, contestants! This week's challenge was "The 19th Century". First up is Donna. Tell us about your tank, Donna.
Donna: Well, Alex, I tried to capture the essence of The Industrial Revolution by pumping coal dust into the water. I think I killed all the fish, but the concept is pure.
Alex Trebek: Interesting. Bob, tell us about your tank.
Bob: All my fish are wearing bustles and bonnets. It's a signature 19th century look.
Alex Trebek: The judges have made a decision. Bob, please hand in your scuba diver ornament.

(*It's been pointed out to me by a couple of people that there was already an American reality show called "Tanked". I'd never heard of it, but apparently it aired on the channel Animal Planet. To clarify, their version was about INSTALLING giant fish tanks; mine is about DECORATING little fish tanks. Plus my show has Alex Trebek while their show's hosts got divorced and the show got cancelled.)

Show 2: Stick It To Me

In this show, the competitors have to make everything out of popsicle sticks.

Alex Trebek: All right, contestants! This week's challenge was "Iconic Buildings". Donna, what happened here?!

Donna: Well, Alex, I tried to recreate the Eiffel Tower, but as anyone who's ever participated in a team-building exercise knows, popsicle sticks aren't stable at great heights, especially when all you have to attach them together is masking tape.

Alex Trebek: That's a shame. Bob, tell me about your structure.

Bob: I built a scale model of the Globe Theatre.

Alex Trebek: Didn't the Globe Theatre burn down?

Bob (*lights match ominously*): That's right, Alex.

Show 3: In the Bag

Who doesn't love homemade purses?

Alex Trebek: I don't understand what I'm still doing here.

Me: You're the host of a reality show that I made up about people creating purses out of everyday household objects.

Alex Trebek: But--

Me: Shhhh. Everything is all right. Just ask about the purses.

Alex Trebek: All right, but this is the last time—I mean it. So the challenge you were given was "purses made from clothing". God, this is dreadful. Donna?

Donna: I cut the bottom off the sleeve of a sweatshirt and hemmed it, adding a piece of cord. It's now a cute satchel.

Alex Trebek (sighs): Bob?

Bob: I made a cunning "manpurse" by cutting the legs off these jeans and hemming the thighs. You can wear it as a fanny pack OR a courier bag.

Alex Trebek: Can I please go back to Jeopardy now?

Me: Okay, but I want to be an answer in the Potpourri category, like "Who is a funny Canadian writer?"

Alex Trebek: You mean "Who is a WEIRD Canadian writer who keeps breaking the 4th wall?

Me: I'm good either way, as long as the answer is Player One.

As an expert on reality shows, I present to you several additional ideas for fantastic reality shows (sans Alex, since he put his foot down), starting with…

1) Cubicle Wars

Host: Hello once again, and welcome to Cubicle Wars, where each week, two co-workers compete to see who can create a stunning office space with little more than a $50 gift card to the Dollar Store and their own imaginations! Let's meet our challengers! This is Jill, a temp worker with a fondness for frogs, as you can see by the many, many statues and stuffies that she has on her desk. Tell us a little bit about yourself, Jill!

Jill: Frogs are amphibians and can speak 7 different languages.

Host: Only one of those things is even correct! Welcome, Jill! And now here's our other contestant, Josh. Josh is an engineer, so no one knows what he actually does!

Josh: That's not true. I—I...

Host: Exactly! Now here are your $50 gift cards. See you next week, you crazy kids!

One week later...

Host: Let's see what Jill and Josh have accomplished. Our live studio audience will then announce the winner!

Audience (which consists of a panhandler that the host found in the lobby): Does anyone have spare change for coffee?

Host: After the show, Stinky Pete! First up is Jill!

Jill: I used my $50 to buy aromatherapy candles and placed them strategically around my cubicle.

Host: That's it? How many candles did you buy?

Jill: 50, obviously. It was the Dollar Store.

Manager (passing by): You can't light those, Jill. I told you, it's a fire hazard.

Jill: FINE, STEVE! But don't come to me when the power goes out, you fascist!

Host: All right—let's see what Josh has done. Ooh, a tiki bar theme! Very nice! I particularly like the inflatable palm tree.

Josh: Thanks. I'm very pleased with the way it turned out, although I've been getting a lot of side-eye because of the torches. THEY'RE

CULTURALLY APPROPRIATE, STEVE! I'M NOT A NAZI!

Host: And now it's that moment we've all been waiting for. Audience, who is our winner?!

Stinky Pete: Is there any whiskey in the tiki bar? NO? Then I pick the candle lady.

Host: Congratulations, Jill. Your prize is that you get to keep all the candles!

Jill: I just want my frogs back. Marcel was teaching me French.

Host: See you next time on Cubicle Wars!

I really think this show has potential. And while I was fleshing it all out, here are some other show ideas I came up with:

2) Souped Up! (a cheaper version of Top Gear)

In this show, two guys take cheap cars and try to make them look cool. With VERY limited resources.

Host: Tell us about today's project, boys.

Gary: It's a 1988 Ford Tempo, base model, beige, with rust accents.

Mitch: We got it for fifty bucks at a yard sale. The upholstery smells like cheese.

Host: And what are your plans for this car?

Gary: No spoilers!

Host: Oh, sorry I asked.

Gary: No, dude—we're not putting a spoiler on it. Spoilers are pretentious.

Mitch: You're goddamned right they're pretentious!

The next day...

Host: Wow! What a transformation. Tell us what you did!

Mitch: We found bigger wheels at the dump and put them on the back. Now it's slanty!

Gary: We used duct tape to make racing stripes. I probably should have used a ruler.

Host: Um...did you put a tow hitch on the back of this car JUST so you could hang a fake scrotum ornament off it?

Mitch: You're goddamned right we did! We made it ourselves out of two oranges and one of Gary's granny's old knee-highs.

Both (high-fiving): Our car has balls, b*tch!

Host: All right then. Join us next week when Gary and Mitch transform a Pinto into a fancy lawn tractor!

Both: Unsafe at any speed!

3) 19 and Counting: Feline Edition

Voice-Over Intro: "Meet Meredith, a 'cat lover', who roams the streets of her town at night, looking for more cats. She has a LOT—maybe more than 19 but who's counting? None of them are actually hers; she stole them all from her neighbours. Her house reeks of urine, but she insists she's 'not crazy'. You be the judge!"

4) Cooking With Wieners

This show is simple. It's just hot dogs. Every week. Audience of at least one (Ken) guaranteed.

5) Flip That Port-a-Potty!

While you might be thinking that this is a decorating show where people take old portable toilets and pretty them up, you're wrong. This show is about Bobby "Flip" Johnson, a real douchecanoe who waits until people go into port-a-potties, then he sneaks up and tips them over. He's killed in episode 3, and the remainder of the season becomes a detective show, where a slightly Asperger's detective and his madcap female sidekick investigate Bobby's murder. Kind of like Jackass meets Elementary. Will we ever find out who killed Bobby? No spoilers!

WHAT ANY NORMAL PERSON WOULD DO

CHAPTER 11: LET'S GET QUIZZICAL

Over the years, I've taken a number of bizarre Facebook quizzes that purport to identify the different aspects of my personality with absolute accuracy. While they are, for the most part, as generic as horoscopes in telling you about what kind of person you are, they are getting more and more desperate for new topics. At first, it was TV characters, like "Which Game of Thrones Character Are You?" or "Which Bond Girl Are You Most Like?" Respectively, I got Arya Stark, and Xenia Onatopp, former Soviet fighter pilot and top assassin. This was very disappointing—I really wanted Daenerys Targaryen, Mother Of F*cking Dragons instead of a whiny little kid who made lists about who she wanted to kill instead of getting revenge by setting people on fire or getting her bad-ass husband to pour molten gold on their heads. Also, I would have preferred Kissy Suzuki, the bad-ass Ninja Bond Girl. Still, it was better than some of the other choices, for example Chew Mee, Holly Goodhead, Plenty O'Toole, or Pussy Galore.

Seriously, am I the only one who thinks that female characters in James Bond movies are named by giggly 12-year-old boys?

"Hey Danny, why don't we name the new Bond Girl 'Perky McBoobs'?"

"Oh my God, dude--hee hee hee--that's AWESOME!!"

"And we'll call the new Bond Villain 'Dick Wanker!'"

"SHHH! Here comes my mom!"

And then they high-five each other and eat cheezies. Yep, that's how Bond characters are named. Anyway, I've been doing these quizzes for a while, and I've come to a couple of conclusions. First, Facebook doesn't know me at all. Over the years, I've been told that my age is 24, that I will have a baby in the very near future (much to Ken's and my collective shock), and that my favourite food is ice cream. Let me just clarify—I'm more than double that age, the only "baby" I currently want comes from either Tiffany's or the Humane Society, and I HATE ice cream with a passion. I don't want to embark on a rant, but why the hell would I want to eat something so cold that I can't taste it? How can Facebook claim to know me if it doesn't realize my favourite food is steak wrapped in bacon?! Which, to anyone who is not a vegetarian, is 'Nature's Perfect Food'?

At any rate, not only are these quizzes seldom accurate, the path to arriving at a conclusion has become so random and convoluted that I swear Facebook is just making this sh*t up. Case in point: I once took a Facebook quiz called "Which Philosopher Are You?" It sounded a little more up-scale than "Which Kardashian Sister Are You?", so I thought I'd give it a whirl:

Question 1: What is the most overrated virtue? Ok, well this sounded somewhat philosophical. There were several options, including Honesty, Faith, and Courage, but I went with Chastity on the grounds that IT'S STUPID. That, friends, is an example of empirical reasoning. Yep, I would definitely have made a great philosopher.

Question 2: Pick a Desperate Housewife. I had NO idea who any of these women were. Would a philosopher actually watch this dreck in the first place? Again, I used my powers of mad logic, and chose a woman whose name began with 'A', because 'A' is the first letter of the alphabet. And the cool thing was that her last name began with 'B'. Angie Bolen. A totally logical choice, even if I had no f*cking clue who she was.

Question 3: Vegetarians are.... There were several choices, mostly negative, like 'Missing out', 'Annoying', or 'More moral than you'. I chose 'Probably right'; the fact is, I would BE a vegetarian if it wasn't for the whole 'steak wrapped in bacon' thing, which I just can't let go of. Question—why do vegetarians eat eggs? Aren't eggs little chickens that never got born? And now you ate them, so they'll never have a fighting chance. I draw my own moral line by not eating lamb or veal for that exact reason. I strongly believe that animals should have the opportunity to cavort and see the world a little before…well, you know. And now, by that same logic, I have to give up eating eggs. Great. Thanks, philosophy.

Question 4: Pick a condiment. I was torn between soya sauce and salsa, but I went with salsa, because if these questions have ANY bearing on what philosopher I'm most like, I'd rather be Che Guevara than Confucius.

Question 5: Worst thing you've ever done? I wasn't copping to anything except Gotten Drunk or Stolen Sweets. I picked stealing candy, because aren't ALL philosophers alcoholics? Drunkenness will not define my philosophy. I stand by that statement. Also, once when I was 4, I took a piece of bubble gum from the variety store. My mom found out and made me go back and apologize to the store owner. It was so mortifying that I pretty much avoided anything illegal from that point on. In fact, I once got caught going through a red light and went to court just so I could tell the judge I was sorry. She reduced my fine—I call that karma. There I go, being all philosophy-ish again.

Question 6: Pick a teen drama. The only one I'd ever seen was Buffy the Vampire Slayer, and even then it was only part of an episode. Maybe this was setting me up to be Vlad the Impaler or something. Was he a philosopher? I'm sure he had a reason why he impaled all those people. Or maybe not. Sometimes philosophy is so f*cking enigmatic.

Question 7: Your ideal Saturday night? I was too distracted at this point by the sidebar headline: "Miley Cyrus wore a prosthetic penis on stage last night", so I randomly picked cooking. I hope to hell

Julia Child was NOT a philosopher.

Question 8: Which European city would you live in? My first reaction was, 'Why isn't Glasgow on this list?! WTF is up with that? Scotland had to have at least ONE philosopher.' So I googled it. There was a list, but I didn't recognize any of the names. Then I saw a picture of Steve Carrell (the American actor) next to someone named Michael Scot, and got suspicious that this site was also run by Facebook.

Question 9: You promised to hang out with your Grandmother tomorrow. What do you do? Some of the options were 'Cook for her and her friends', 'Cancel at the last minute', or 'Grin and bear it'. Unfortunately, my grandmother passed away a couple of decades ago, so I chose 'Look forward to catching up'.

Question 10: Right now I am…. At this point, I had no idea how any of these random and absurd questions could lead to any particular philosopher except for Jean-Paul Sartre, so I chose 'Confused'.

The program calculated my responses and came up with this: "You got: Jean-Jacques Rousseau. Although you believe in individual freedom, you think that social contracts are necessary in order to allow society to function in a rational, non-impulsive way." Close enough, Facebook, and in true philosophical fashion, I have logically concluded that it was my choice of Angie Bolen that led to this revelation.

I still had a little time to kill so I did the next quiz on the page which was "What Fossil Are You?" I went through the series of questions: Pick a vacation plan (visit a castle), pick a pattern (psychedelic), pick a moment from Drakes' Hotline Bling video (WTF? Random.), pick a Greek goddess (Athena), pick outdated 90s slang (Aight), pick a moustache (Old West saloon keeper), pick a geologic time period (Ordivician, because it sounds Illuminati-ish and cool). I got this:

"You are just like an ammonite! These awesome looking sea-critters were everywhere back in the day, but not much is known about their behavior. Like them, you are elegant as f*ck, but also seductively mysterious. People have been known to frame ammonites' likeness on the walls of their majestic mansions and palatial villas and the same will certainly be said of you one day."

"Elegant as f*ck" and totally philosophical. Yep, that's me, all right.

I've also done an inordinate amount of 'Holiday Quizzes', mostly because I love decorating magazines and they always try to help you define your 'personal style' when it comes to Christmas decorating and I love it when anyone assumes that I actually HAVE a style to unwrap, like there's a part of me just DYING to run into a forest and gather evergreen boughs and whatnot. The explanation under the headline in last year's magazine was, "If determining your home's holiday look is your own personal nightmare before Christmas, fear not. We're here to help." Personal nightmare?! Aren't we getting a little dramatic here? Because the nightmares I have focus on the house burning down or worldwide pandemics, not so much on whether people appreciate my decorating style. But the magazine thoughtfully provided a list of 10 questions to help me determine exactly how to discover my "festive style" by giving me four choices—A, B, C, or D, and then adding up the choices to correspond with a style. Here we go:

1) Which winter wreath would you hang?

I chose D, the "Feathery Evergreen", except that I would forgo the peacock feathers and bow, and add twinkle lights. Now it looks just like the wreaths that Ken and I hang in our windows every year. We keep them in a closet under the stairs along with the twenty extension cords we need to make them light up.

2) Choose the prettiest gift wrap.

While "Snowflake Chic" and "Golden Glamour" were both very fetching, I myself am partial to "Last Year's Leftovers" with a side of "Scotch Tape and a Bit of Ribbon".

3) What's Your Must-Watch Christmas Movie?

I'd only seen one out of the 4 choices—A Christmas Story, which is so wonderfully random with the leg lamp and the pack of dogs that continually appear out of nowhere to wreak havoc. As for the other options, It's a Wonderful Life is way too morbid, A Muppet Christmas is way too Muppet-y, and I've never actually seen Love Actually. MY must-watch movie is How the Grinch Stole Christmas. Not the live action film, which is ridiculously over the top, but the original animated classic, which I can recite almost verbatim, having watched it every year since I was old enough to remember. It's tradition, and I don't care if it messes up my style score. Also, Die Hard WASN'T on the list, which frankly is ridiculous because it's the best Christmas movie of all time. Yippee Ki Yay indeed.

4) Which candles will you set out this season?

While "a selection of unscented tea lights and votives in mercury glass containers" sounds quite glam, I'm gonna go with NONE, because as I previously mentioned, one of my personal nightmares is having the house burn down, and candles are tiny fires that aspire to be bigger ones, in my book. Don't get me wrong—I HAVE candles but I only use them when the power is out and I can see them in the dark.

5) Which wallpaper would you use for an accent wall?

What? Now I'm putting up wallpaper?! Go to hell.

6) Select a pair of holiday pajamas

Now, this I can get behind. I'm going to pick…a

"monogrammed crisp white button-down nightshirt and matching pants"? Nooo. "A long sleep tee featuring a flamingo donning a Santa hat"? Nooo. Okay, these choices are NOT appealing to me. I shall choose the reindeer patterned flannel pants I bought last summer on sale, accented with a Joe Fresh tank top in "used to be crisp white but then I washed it with a black hoodie and now it's kind of grey and I only wear it to bed".

7) Your Yuletide tree is…

Whichever one is closest to where we parked the car at the tree farm. The magazine's option D is "An imperfect long-needled pine, chopped fresh from the forest", so I kind of won this one except that in recent years we've been buying small potted trees that we can replant in our yard in the spring rather than going into the forest, finding the biggest tree and chopping it down with…a herring (that's your Monty Python reference for this chapter) . The best part of the tree question is option C, the picture of a "life-like" tree that you can buy from Canadian Tire for $500. I can get a whole decade's worth of real trees for that price, imperfect though they may be.

8) Pick an ornament.

One of the choices is a felt ketchup bottle. It's thirteen dollars. I can't even. I've used the same vintage glass ornaments from the early twentieth century for the last twenty-ish years. I also make my own ornaments to give out to friends and family made from wood. On a more serious note, I choose a word each year to burn into them--this year's word is HOPE because I think we all need a little bit of that.

And now, to finish up this volume, I have a series of quizzes that I've offered my readers over the years, and if you read this book carefully, there's a good chance you'll get most of the answers correct!

Business Quiz

Once, I was shopping in a local strip mall and as I was leaving, I noticed another business in the plaza, a hair salon. It was called The Main Attraction Hair Studio. And all I could think is, 'There's a missed opportunity if ever I saw one'. Like, who was the genius who said, "I know that the word 'Mane' is another word for long, luxurious hair, but if we call it "The Mane Attraction", nobody is going to get THAT"? It's like having the last name Taylor and being a seamstress, but calling your business 'Tailor-Made'. I mean, why would you NOT capitalize on the obvious?!

And while I was taking a break from writing so I could think of more examples, I asked Kate for help:

Me: What are some other fun plays on words that people could use for their businesses?

Kate: Um…Sofa King.

Me: I don't get it…

Kate: Because their sofas are so f*cking comfortable.

Me: (laughs hysterically)

And I remember when I was a kid, being absolutely fascinated by the Dew Drop Inn, a motel in the cottage town we used to visit. I don't think I would have been quite as impressed if the name had been the Do Drop Inn, although that's kind of cute too. Of course, if I owned a motel, it would be called the Come Inn…and it's no wonder that people think I'm talking about sex stuff all the time. At any rate, I started thinking of some other fun names for businesses and I designed this quiz. You have to match the names with the businesses. And just to up the ante, all the names I made up kind of sound like porn shops, so you have to guess which one is actually a porn shop. Also, one of them is a real business name that I found online, so you have to figure that out too. Answers are below:

Business Names

1) Let's Get Fizz-ical
2) We're Going To Pump You Up
3) One Man's Junk
4) The Hole Shebang
5) Can You Dig It
6) He Shoots, He Scores
7) Quality Tools
8) We Suck
9) Big Ass Slabs

10) Pour Some Sugar On Me

Types of Businesses

a) Excavating Company

b) Sporting Goods

c) Donut Store

d) Confectioners

e) Chainsaw Milling and Timberwork – this is a real company, I sh*t you not

f) Tire Repair

g) Vacuum Repair Service

h) Adult Novelties i.e. porn

i) Soda Shop

j) Thrift Store

Answers: 1i, 2f, 3j, 4c, 5a, 6b, 7h, 8g, 9e, 10d

Did you get the porn store name correct? If not, no worries—they're all pretty porn-y.

Speaking of porn, I created a quiz one day after we had a neighbour come over to visit. We had just redecorated our bedroom, adding some architectural columns and whatnot and she was interested in seeing the end result. I proudly escorted her into the room where she looked around and complimented me on the new design, but I thought she seemed a little lukewarm and anxious to leave. Then, on our way out, I glanced over at the bed and gasped internally. Ken had wrapped one of our dog's tug toys around one of his big rubber bones, and from a distance, it looked very much like something you would find in an "adult" store. I wanted to run after her as she hurried downstairs, holding it aloft and exclaiming, "It's for the dog!!" but I don't think that would have helped matters any, and may, in fact, have made them worse. But then I got looking around my house and realized that a LOT of the dog's toys look like they may have come from The Stag Shop, which is the most common sex toy franchise around here. So with that in mind, I tried to make up a quiz called 'Sex Toy or Dog Toy?' The only problem? All dog toys look like sex toys. Don't believe me? Take a good hard look at any of the rubber toys your dog plays with and TELL ME I'M WRONG.

Sheep/Goat Fence or Kitten?

This quiz is something I created after seeing an ad on Facebook Marketplace. The ad was for a 'Temporary Sheep/Goat Fence' but the only picture accompanying the ad was a photo of a kitten being held in someone's hand. When I saw the picture, I thought it was strange, because apparently you're not allowed to sell pets on Facebook Marketplace, but then I saw the description and realized that this was, in fact, NOT a pet but a very skilled little feline who was worth every penny of his $123.00 price tag.

Now, it never occurred to me that you could use a kitten for the purpose of coralling sheep and/or goats, just like it never occurred to me that you should hold a kitten like it's an ice cream cone, but then I gave it a little more thought. I came up with this clever quiz for you to demonstrate how much a kitten has in common with a sheep/goat fence. You need to read the items on the following list and decide whether they apply to kittens, sheep/goat fences, or both:

1) Can be used to keep out sheep and/or goats
2) Adorable
3) Comes in a variety of colours
4) Might have fleas
5) Needs lots of maintenance
6) Enjoys the outdoors
7) Potentially electrified
8) Poops in a box
9) Hisses if you try to cross it
10) Vomits on your rug
11) Kills birds and small rodents
12) Very long
13) Metal or wood

OK, let's see how you did.

Exclusively kittens: #8 and #10. Exclusively sheep/goat fences: #13. Both: All the rest.

Now, you may be saying, "I don't think—" but I'm going to interrupt you in order to explain.

1) "Can be used to keep out sheep/goats". According to the ad, this kitten CAN be used to keep out sheep and/or goats, and I take the word of the expert who owns the kitten and not some book reader who owns a sheep and/or goat farm, KEVIN. Also, the ad says it's a TEMPORARY fence; otherwise, using a kitten as a permanent sheep/goat fence would be very unrealistic.

2) "Adorable". I have seen MANY adorable sheep/goat fences in my time. In fact, just the other day, Ken and I were driving around the countryside and he said, "Look at that cute fence" and I said, "We should stop and take a picture of it" and we did, because it was adorable.

3) "Comes in a variety of colours". I mean obviously sheep/goat fences don't come in as MANY colours as kittens, but they come in several shades of gray or brown, so that counts.

4) "Might have fleas". I said "Might".
5) "Needs lots of maintenance". Fences and kittens are both high-maintenance, what with their potential for rust and needing to be amused constantly.

6) "Enjoys the outdoors". This is obviously true of both because sheep/goat fences live in the outdoors, which they wouldn't if they didn't enjoy it, I would hope, and kittens are always making a run for the door to get out of your house.

7) "Potentially electrified". I said "Potentially". Also, what do you think makes a kitten's fur stand on end? And have you ever touched your kitten and gotten a shock? I rest my case.

8) "Poops in a box". I don't think sheep\goat fences defecate, and if they did, I can't see a farmer providing them a box to do it in. Although you never know with farmers.

9) "Hisses if you try to cross it". This one is predicated on the sheep/goat fence being electrified. In which case, it's true of both. It's also true of the Canada Goose, affectionately known as the Evil Lake Chicken.

10) "Vomits on your rug". This could never be true of a sheep/goat fence because you wouldn't have one in your house with access to a rug. Unless you also keep sheep and/or goats in your house, and then it would be like a baby gate or something, and I still can't see it vomiting on the rug, although the sheep and/or goats might. But if you've ever owned a kitten, you know they do this all the damn time, and especially when you have company over for dinner, and right as you start eating, the kitten comes in, makes an unearthly yowling

sound, and pukes on the rug. Kittens have impeccable timing, which they also have in common with sheep/goat fences. I should have put that on the list.

11) "Kills birds and small rodents". This is also predicated on the sheep/goat fence being electrified. It also depends on the voltage. Ken has touched electric fences before but he's not home right now, so I'll ask him later if he thinks it could electrocute a field mouse. Update: Ken says that the voltage probably wouldn't kill them but would give them a good jolt, so I'm changing 11 to "Wounds birds and small rodents".

12) "Very long". I've seen long kittens. Fight me.

13) "Metal or wood". There's no way I can stretch this to make it apply to kittens, at least not the living kind, so I'm giving number 13 to sheep/goat fences.

Overall, as you can see, kittens and sheep/goat fences DO have a lot in common, so I think the person who posted the ad should be asking a hell of a lot more than $123.00. A much better deal than the ad for used rocks at a dollar a piece.

Final Quiz About Tools: Match the tool with the description.

a) Dirt Tosser
b) Hitty Thing

WHAT ANY NORMAL PERSON WOULD DO

c) Marathon Man

d) Ho

e) Stabby Bastard

f) You'll Shoot Your Eye Out

g) Reverse Autumnal Vacuum

h) No. F*ck No.

i) How Did I Cut The Cord On This Thing WITH This Thing AGAIN?! Goddammit.

j) The One With The Square End

Here are the answer choices. Try to match them and see how well you do!

1) Exacto Knife

2) Robertson Screwdriver

3) Hoe

4) Hedge Trimmer

5) Staple Gun/Nail Gun/Red Ryder BB Gun

6) Shovel

7) Table Saw That Ken Removed The Safety Guard From

8) Hammer

9) Drill

10) Leaf Blower

Correct Answers: A6, B8, C9, D3, E1, F5, G10, H7, I4, J2.

How many did you get correct? Remember, there are a lot of tools out there and it's important to know them when you see them!

Well, that's the end of the book. I hope you enjoyed reading it as much as I've enjoyed writing it, because writing funny sh*t is cathartic for me, and now I can go to sleep happy. And then wake up at 11:34 pm to plan for a potential earthquake.

Temporary Sheep/Goat Fence
$123

ABOUT THE AUTHOR

Award-winning writer Suzanne Craig-Whytock is the author of four novels, *Smile*, *The Dome*, *The Seventh Devil*, and *The Devil You Know*

(Bookland Press), and two short story collections, *Feasting Upon The Bones* and *At The End Of It All* (Potter's Grove Press). Her short fiction and poetry have appeared in numerous literary journals, and she regularly publishes essays focused on life's absurdities under the pen name 'Mydangblog'. She is also the Editor of DarkWinter Literary Magazine, an online journal which publishes short stories and poetry from both emerging and established writers, as well as the founder of DarkWinter Press.

Manufactured by Amazon.ca
Bolton, ON